Blue Horses Rush In

Volume 34

SUN TRACKS

An American Indian Literary Series

Series Editor
Ofelia Zepeda

Editorial Committee
Vine Deloria, Jr.
Larry Evers
Joy Harjo
N. Scott Momaday
Emory Sekaquaptewa
Leslie Marmon Silko

Blue Horses Rush In

POEMS AND STORIES

Luci Tapahonso

THE UNIVERSITY OF ARIZONA PRESS • TUCSON

THE UNIVERSITY OF ARIZONA PRESS

www.uapress.arizona.edu

Library of Congress Cataloging-in-Publication Data
Tapahanso, Luci
Blue horses rush in : poems and stories / Luci Tapahonso.
p.   cm. — (Sun tracks ; v. 34)
ISBN 978-0-8165-1728-2 (pbk. : alk. paper)
1. Navajo Indians—Literary collections. I. Title. II. Series.
PS501.S35   vol. 34
YPS3570.A567"
810.8'0054 S—DC21
[811'.54] 96-45896
CIP

The story "White Bead Girl" contains an excerpt from "Furious
Versions," © 1990 by Li-Young Lee. Reprinted from *The City in
Which I Love You* by Li-Young Lee, with the permission of BOA
Editions, Ltd., 260 East Avenue, Rochester, New York 14604.

Manufactured in the United States of America on acid-free,
archival-quality paper, and processed chlorine free.

16   15   14   13   12   8   7   6   5   4

For our children,
Misty Ortiz; Amber, Jonathan, and
Derek Martin; and Lori Tapahonso

and granddaughters, Briana Nezbah
and Chamisa Bah

Contents

Preface

On a bright Sunday afternoon, we sat outside my parents' home in Ship-rock. There was a little breeze but no dust, and it was very warm. Around Shiprock everyone hoped for rain, but I had just come from Kansas, where it had been raining for three days straight, and for me the warm dry air was refreshing. Years ago, one of my older sisters bought our father a heavily padded patio chair, and he sat comfortably in it now, his walker within reach. In his old age, one of his greatest pleasures is to sit under the trees in the warmth of the afternoon and watch his great-grandchildren and various dogs, cats, and birds play. Two sisters, one of our daughters and two sons (my sisters' children), and I sat with our parents in a semicircle of benches and plastic chairs.

We sat for hours — talking, laughing, and sharing family memories and stories. The conversation switched easily between Diné and English and, at times, a rhythmic blending of the two. Our father told us how a man called "ashdla'" (five) and a relative we call "sałii," which means "speedy," were given their names. We all smiled because "Speedy" does not describe sałii, who's now in his late fifties. The kids talked about school — one of the boys had won first place for building a solar-powered car, and we told him it was the influence of his little father, sałii, who used to race around in the mountains raising dust on dirt roads . One of our older sons was home from Fort Lewis College where he is a senior. He was relieved to be home, having had enough of cafeteria food and dorm life. Although my own children were not with us in Shiprock, their names and presences were interwoven throughout the conversation as we talked of their childhoods, their college course work, or Lori's children. The topics that afternoon ranged from the funniest of stories to more serious topics.

That morning I had been dismayed to read the obituary of a high school friend in the newspaper. It was doubly disheartening to learn that she had died from cirrhosis of the liver. She was intelligent and pretty, and I had always admired her for being on the honor roll without much effort. She, like many other bright young people we grew up with, had gotten caught in the turmoil that alcoholism wreaks on otherwise stable families. She and I lost contact after high school, but that afternoon, we mourned informally by remembering her, her many sisters, her parents, and her grandparents. I discovered through the stories that she was related to us — her family came from the same area near Red Valley. My mother talked about my deceased friend's grandfather and how people remembered him. Her old grandfather had had an amusing name, and another humorous story lay behind it.

Late that afternoon, a huge whirlwind suddenly whipped up the north side of the house, veering east in between my sister's mobile home and the house, hurling leaves, dirt, small branches, and bits of debris about eight feet into the air. The dogs jumped up from their sleep and dashed out of the way. We yelled out in surprise as the whirlwind rushed past. It turned north and moved in a straight line another twenty yards or so, then shifted back toward us. My mother reacted quickly and shouted "Naadaaní!" in a scolding voice. Just as rapidly, it turned east and swept over the road and the irrigation ditch away from us. We laughed about how she frightened it by shouting out, "Your in-law!" In the Diné traditional way, direct contact between a woman and her sons-in-law is forbidden, so family members warn them by saying "Naadaaní!" if they are likely to encounter each other. Then usually the son-in-law leaves the room immediately. "It's just an old-time Navajo," my mother said afterward of the whirlwind. The event led to more interesting stories about what whirlwinds represent to different people.

That afternoon was like countless other times when my family members gather. Sometimes it is just my mother and me at the kitchen table, talking quietly. Oftentimes during school vacations various generations of the family congregate in my mother's kitchen and living room. We stay awake into the early morning—talking, laughing, eating, putting together puzzles, sharing photo albums, playing games, and simply enjoying the presence of family.

Appointment books, telephones, faxes, cellular phones, and e-mail are literally a world away during those times. Linear time doesn't matter. We are awakened by the bright New Mexico sun, and days pass without any rushing about. My parents may have medical appointments or various errands, but these activities are done in the same relaxed manner. We meet relatives or friends almost everywhere, and conversations consist of jokes, stories, and intricate wordplay. Before we head home, we stop at the flea market for a roasted mutton sandwich and a cup of coffee. My father's niece, Elsie Henry, has an excellent Navajo menu and always sends a free bowl of stew and frybread for Daddy, who is her father also. If Elsie's stand is closed, someone always knows who else makes "really good" mutton sandwiches.

To leave Shiprock is difficult. After an hour or so of saying good-bye, as we drive out of the front yard there is always a group of family members waving and watching us leave. As we drive through Shiprock, we encounter other family members, friends, or relatives at the 7-Eleven, the gas station, or at City Market. So we stop once more to catch up on the latest news and say good-bye again. They ask several times when we'll be coming home next. We pass one of my brothers on the farm highway, honk, then pull over. We aren't sure if he knows it's us, but he says he

can tell a rental car from "way off." We're driving a "bilagáana bichidí"—
a white person's car—definitely not a Ford or Chevy pickup. He parks
alongside us off the road, and again we settle into a "talking" mode. We all
get out of the car, crowd around the truck windows, and talk and laugh
together. Then he and his son get out, put down the tailgate, and we sit
talking as traffic passes by. The kids play in the dirt beside us or in the
truck bed behind us. We know almost everyone who drives by. My brother
tells us little things about different people as they pass. Finally, we *have* to
leave ("for reals," as the kids say), and once again we shake hands or hug
each other and get back into our conspicuous rental car.

My younger sister and her daughter ride with us to Rehoboth, where
they live, east of Gallup, and we continue to Albuquerque, another two-
and-one-half hours. Even in Albuquerque, there is an assortment of
friends and relatives whom we meet for coffee or lunch, and the storytell-
ing continues, though it is more formal and usually in English.

Thus, as we return east to Kansas, the mode of conversation, the words,
and the languages shift. By the time we reach Oklahoma, we know we
are not in New Mexico—the wind may now be humid, or it's raining,
and when we speak to people at restaurants or gas stations, they usually
say, "Pardon me?" or "Excuse me?" Our Navajo accents are still thick. We
know this, and we smile as we repeat things.

This transition in language and conversation usually continues for the
first two or three days we are back in Lawrence. Soon the accent lessens,
but never disappears entirely. In Lawrence, we gather in our home in the
evenings or on weekends—our two daughters and their little families—
and exchange stories from our visit.

"Tell us everything that happened!" they insist.

"Well, I got to Shiprock late, but your Grandma was still up. She had
mutton stew with corn and yeast bread ready . . ." I begin.

Our conversation is punctuated with laughter and with Navajo expressions like "aye-e!" or "yahdilah!" Sometimes we simply become quiet with homesickness.

In retelling stories, it's clear to listeners—my children in this case—who the speakers are, or who the story concerns. Obvious advantages of oral storytelling are the expressions of the teller, the responses of the participants, and the gestures as well as the inflections in the voices. Although many of the stories or jokes that are told can be translated and relayed fairly well in written form, the clear sense of voices and characters is diminished in some ways, so that even though it's obvious when I tell a story orally that I'm not the protagonist or other person, the reader of a story may interpret it otherwise.

Many times in the critiques of poems and stories, I, as author, have been assumed to be the character in the work. Perhaps because the atmosphere is paramount, when one hears these stories, there is an immense affection and acceptance of all present, and most important, there is a deep respect and love for language, both Navajo and English. The greatest delights in these sessions are imaginative and clever wordplay and the subtle uses of humor and silence at crucial moments. These aspects of the stories are understood without the use of words. Perhaps it is this sense of immediacy and the memory of my own emotional responses the first time I heard a particular story, which influence the way characters or speakers are presented, that causes some readers to assume that the story is autobiographical. This occurs so often now that I find myself explaining repeatedly, "If all the things I write about happened to me, I would never have the time actually to write anything."

Rather, this book is a combination of my observations and experiences and those of friends and relatives, or of persons I may not even know. Many Diné stories begin with the expression, "'ałk' idą́ą́' jiní" (a long time they said) if the event requires it; otherwise, they start with "Jiní" or "they said," and who "they" are is not questioned, because inherent in Diné storytelling is the belief that, indeed, the events or the story did occur at some time in the past. There is not an insistence on "facts" or "evidence." The understanding is that the function of stories is to entertain and that they usually involve some teaching as well as the exploration of possibilities, besides which they all require a vivid imagination and a non-judgmental mind-set. Therefore, one may get caught up in the story, on some level becoming a part of it, and even more intensely so as it is retold at another time. Perhaps it is this "active" participation on my part that leads readers to view my work as wholly autobiographical. Of course, this conjecture by scholars and critics conflicts with the literary tenet that one should not assume that the speaker in a poem or story is the writer, and it's interesting that this situation arises only when the stories are written in English.

This collection embodies in many ways the essence of the Diné love of language and stories. Some of the stories are humorous, while others are intensely sad accounts of loss and grief. Many of them were originally told in Diné, taking no longer than ten minutes in the telling. Yet in recreating them, it is necessary to describe the land, the sky, the light, and other details of time and place. In this way, I attempt to create and convey the setting for the oral text. In writing, then, I revisit the place or places concerned and try to bring the reader to them, thereby enabling myself and other Navajos to sojourn mentally and emotionally to our home, Dinétah.

My intent is to share the concern and empathy that my parents and kin feel for the land, for each other, for the children, and for those in despair. The book is dedicated to my granddaughters, Chamisa Bah and Briana Nezbah, who show us over and over the instinctive delight of songs and stories with which we were all born. Because of them, I am reassured that the old cycles of singing and talking in the way that is distinctly Navajo will continue. This book is also for their great-grandparents, who remind us continually of our histories, and who have instilled in us, their children, the love of language upon which our lives have always depended.

Acknowledgments

I would like to give special thanks to my family and friends, especially Vangie Parsons Yazzie, Della Toadlena, Fredericka John, Emmett White, and Louis Owens.

I am grateful to the Hall Center for the Humanities at the University of Kansas, the Phoenix (Arizona) Arts Commission, and the Frost Place in Franconia, New Hampshire, for grants that aided in the compilation of this book.

Blue Horses Rush In

Shisóí

For Briana Nezbah Edmo, born October 22, 1992

She was born on a bright fall afternoon,
already chubby, and quivering with wetness.
She gasped for air, and for her mother's warm body.

Her name is She-Who-Brings-Happiness because upon being carried,
she instinctively settles into the warmth
of your shoulder and neck.
She nestles, like a little bird, into the contours of your body.
All you can say is, "She's so sweet, I don't know what to do."
And we smile, beaming with pleasure.

She sleeps, even breaths and milky sighs just below your ear.
Other times she snuggles into you and watches
with bright, dark eyes. It feels so much like the trust
we have somehow forgotten over the years.
All you can do is kiss her warm forehead and say,
"She's so sweet, I don't know what to do."

Sometimes when I haven't seen her for a day, or even a week,
she runs to me, her arms straight out for balance,
and hugs my legs. "My gahma," she murmurs into my skirt.
Then she holds her arms up and says, "Eh, eh,"
and I pick her up; she snuggles into me, sighing.

Then I tell her, "No shinaa, shiyázhí, shisóí, ho shił nizhóní."
My little one, my daughter's child, what happiness you are to me.
She cries a little, ah, ah, like the infant
she no longer is, and I hold her like the sweet surprise
she will always be. We sit like that a while, and then she hums,
"Hey na yah." I take the hint and sing the old lullaby
her great-grandmother sang to the child I once was.

She shifts in my lap saying, "Star, star."
We turn to the twinkling Christmas lights still up in July,
and sing, "Twinkle, twinkle little star."
She falls asleep, and I hand her to her mother,
saying, "She's so sweet, I don't know what to do."

Now each time she toddles into the room, we turn and say,
"Ahshénee shiyázhí. You want some juice? How about milk?"
She-Who-Brings-Happiness smiles and climbs onto the nearest lap.
As she snuggles comfortably into the circle around the table,
we murmur, "She's so sweet, we don't know what to do."

A Song for the Direction of North

Tsaile, Arizona

The sky is a blanket of stars covering all of us.
The night is folding darkness girl.

Just after midnight, we walk in the cool mountain air.
The stars glisten so.
Their bright beauty makes us dizzy.
Laughing, we bump lightly against each other.
I hold my daughter's arm.
We walk slowly, still looking at the sky.
The night is folding darkness girl.

Those few stars in the north seem so close.
Maybe they are right above Buffalo Pass.
Underneath the stars, the Lukachukai Mountain
lies dark and quiet.
It breathes with the sacred wind.
Clearly, clearly the barking of dogs echoes from miles away.
Right there under the pine trees,
the shiny, smooth horses snort and breathe loudly.
The night is folding darkness girl.

The Milky Way stretches wide and careless across the dark night.
It is a bright sash belt with thin, soft edges.
The night is scattered thickly with glistening specks
and blinking orbs of light.

In some night spaces, there is no order.
"Coyote sure did a good job," Misty says.
We laugh, and I love my daughters so.
The night is folding darkness girl.

The house sits strong and round against the base of the mountain.
In the dark stillness, slants of moon and starlight
wait within the curved walls for white dawn girl.
Slants of light wait for white dawn boy.

Ahshénee 'wéé, t'áá kóó neiit'aash dooleełée.
My beloved baby, if only we could stay here.
There is no end to this clear, sweet air.
To the west, immense rocks lie red and stark in the empty desert.
Somewhere my daughters' smooth laughter
deepens the old memory of stars.

Each night, I become Folding Darkness Girl.
Each night, I become Folding Darkness Boy.
Each morning, White Bead Girl arrives.
Each morning, White Bead Boy arrives.

ʼAhídzískéíí

It's not a grand thing after all,
just that warm comfort in murmuring "good night"
before I sink into that dark quiet
that exists only when we're together.

Otherwise, when I'm traveling,
the same 'good night' on the phone,
and I listen intently (for what I'm not sure),
leave a light on for safety, drift off to sleep, half-listening;
a little noise and I'm sitting up in bed, surveying the room,
sometimes even the entire block from the hotel window.
I rush to the phone and double check,
should I dial 0 or 8–911?
I check the locks again, then lie back down
afraid to sleep, yet wanting to sleep, knowing
that fatigue will be obvious in the morning.
I've had so much practice.

When we're together, checking locks doesn't occur to me,
local crime seems so far away (never mind
that we are in the heart of the city),
I insist upon complete darkness, and what I am sure of
is that if I turn over, your warm chest or arms will surround me.
That should I awaken, confused as to where I am (once again),
you will reach for me knowing exactly how to reassure me.

And when we drink coffee together
in this bright California morning,
mountains towering around us, I move closer to knowing
what the Creator means by "nizhónígo 'ahídzískéii."
They are sitting beside each other in a house of beauty.

Tsaile April Nights

Earlier today, thin sheets of red dirt
folded into the dark mountain
blown up from the western desert floor.
       You know,
       the whole, empty Navajo spaces around
       Many Farms, Chinle, Round Rock.

Later, light rain slanted into the valley.
The female paused for an hour or so.
She sat and watched us awhile,
then clouds of mist waited until evening and left
The male rain must have been somewhere over the mountain,
near Cove or Beclabito, chasing children and puppies indoors.
But here, the quiet snow will move in
       a newborn breathing
       those first new nights.

The lake is frozen,
a glazed white plate suspended in the dark.

I long to hear your voice.
       Hushed, deep murmurs in the cold quiet,
       and low laughter echoing in the still.

I like to sleep with piñon smoke.
The cold dry air chills my skin, my breath.
    Stories descend into the dark,
    warm, light circles.

In Praise of Texas

So many times I've rushed into airports frazzled,
my hair everywhere as I lugged bags along,
my face flushed from hurrying,
and my breathing loud and raspy.

But I will never be seen like that in Texas.

Because George Strait lives in Texas.
A friend saw him once at Gate 29 at Dallas-Fort Worth.
He is so nice, she said, and to prove it,
she handed me a picture.
George Strait had his arm around her. He was smiling.
I struggled so to share her happiness.

Though that was years ago, I believe that unending faith
precedes glittering possibilities.
I believe that the world is basically good,
and so I am certain that one day
I will just happen to run into George Strait in Texas.
Maybe he'll be buying the *Dallas Morning News* at a Circle K.
Maybe as I'm having a salad, he'll walk into the same cafe,
like an ordinary person, and order a medium Diet Coke.

Each time I am in Texas,
my hair shines radiant,
I won't allow dark thoughts to mar my face even for an instant,
my hat has been steamed and re-shaped,
my clothes are smooth and coordinated,
and I am never rushed.

Once as we dined alongside the Riverwalk in San Antonio,
my husband smiled at me and said, "You sure are pretty."
"Thanks honey," I said, "but do you really mean it,
or are you just saying that?"
"I really mean it," he said.
I removed my sunglasses and searched his face
in the evening light,
but I couldn't tell if he really meant it.
In any case, I glanced around very discreetly to see
if anyone else (maybe a country western singer)
shared his sentiment. Just in case, I reminded
myself to sit up straight.

No way.
You'll never see me looking frazzled
or the least bit scuzzy in Texas.
Whether we drive through Dalhart, visit Fort Worth
for a few days, take in a Rangers game,
or whether I have a brief layover at Houston-Hobby,
I believe that one has to be prepared
for whatever Texas has to offer.

Sometimes as the plane glides over that vast, plain state,
above scattered herds of horses, I can see the luster
sparkling off their broad backs like intense hope and I am
reassured that dreams can blossom without any urging on our part.

Starlore

No one could have told me that growing older could be this way: that children would turn on parents and disappear into gritty border towns, or run the abandoned downtown streets of Denver or Phoenix; that families could split into hardened circles over one sentence uttered in anger; that sons and daughters would leave with friends for Europe or New York; that they would leave for boot camp, or a college where they are one of five Indian students, and that parents would not know all they endured. Yet through these instances and many more, we address our fears in ways that have never changed.

On this June night, we gather at our parents' home and leave in a caravan of nine cars, a string of headlights across the flat desert to the home of the man who will listen and help us. It is almost midnight when we park outside his hooghan, the round ceremonial house. We enter slowly, clockwise, then sit on the smooth, cool ground. Above the flickering fire in the center of the hooghan, we see clouds rushing by through the chimney hole. The wind whistles through the opening. It makes us hope for rain. The family has filled the hooghan. We whisper among ourselves until he arrives—the one who knows the precise songs, the long, rhythmic prayers that will restore the world for us.

Later we follow him outside where the stars
glimmer in the black sky.
Then a single star shatters; sparkling streams of light
trail downward and disappear.

The star remains whole and glowing.
"This has happened for all of you," he says.

To the south, the moon passes behind luminous, billowing
rain clouds. Below us, the dark river echoes in the valley;
small rocks tumble alongside and underneath the roaring water.
The night is filled with the damp riverbank
and sweet approaching rain.

    Each night I think of this as darkness moves in,
    casting shadows at first, then immersing us
    in the clean night air.
    I think of this as the moon glides slowly from east
    to west among the distant stars.
    Because of this, I understand that I am valued.
    Because of the years I have lived, I am valued.
    Yes, I am pitied by the huge sky,
    the bright moon, and glittering stars.
    We consist of long, breathless songs of healing.
    We are made of prayers that have no end.

    I have seen the stars separate.
    And I am, I am.

I Know It

Taylor Ranch, New Mexico/December 1988

He is trapped
on the east side of the Sandias.
The snow is deep and dry.
Roads have disappeared
      or are made visible by stranded cars askew.
      Weary people wave for help.

He is there
trapped in a study with a computer;
words and bits of conversation swirl silently.
He traps them forever with the steady click of fingertips

No phone,
no little squares of pink yelling,
      "Call me, call me,"
      "Meeting at two,"
      "Can't make class,"—signed: ill or dying student.
He is trapped in luxury, I think.

It's snowing in suburbia this morning.
We plunge into hysteria;
delay school, watch ice on bridges and overpasses,
cancel a.m. kindergarten, stay home if at all possible.

I will.
I refuse to drive off this rise of land
and mingle with people who drive like me.

The dog is happy, catching flakes in his mouth.
His history is snow, sleds, tracking elk, deer and caribou.
He runs back and forth, panting loudly.
He wants me to watch his celebration.

From the top level of the backyard,
the city below hums steadily
and the Sandias rise into clouds.
There is no separation between
the heavy sky and sheer rock.

A solid gray looms over the valley from where I sit.
In between, the dog races his happiness silly.

In 1990, the Phoenix Arts Commission assembled

a collaborative team of photographers and writers

to interpret the history and development of an

ancient Hohokamki[1] settlement and the most important

Columbian canals in the New World. The one-thousand-year

ruin was initially unearthed in 1900 and designated

a national landmark in 1964. The team documented

the effects of the construction of the Hohokam Expressway,

which cut through extensive, previously unknown villages,

near the site of the present Pueblo Grande Museum

in east Phoenix. The following four pieces

are part of an exhibition of photographs and accompanying prose.[2]

Rain in the Desert

Rain in the desert is overwhelmingly beautiful—
the early morning scents of dirt and wet plants.
Streets in the city shine with a newness
and streams of water rush along the gutters,
disappearing under the city to some unknown place.
People drive slower than usual in the crisp air.
At eight o'clock on Saturday morning, everything slows,
and people have their car windows open.
The morning is languid and clean—
the heat of the day remote—
held somewhere in the mountains east of Phoenix.
There, hundreds of miles away, the White Mountain people
move around in the almost cold morning,
drinking coffee outside and cooking breakfast over an open fire.

At the Pueblo Grande Museum, thin muddy rain rushes into steel grates
designed to help protect the archaeological site. Beneath the newly
represerved and reconstructed mound, metal pipes stretch along narrow
spaces that connect nearby to the city drainage system, which is invisible.
We know it exists; we have seen the square grates set around the mound.
To the south, a few hundred yards away, homeless people set out
containers to catch a bit of rainwater.

How must the remaining spirits of the Hohokamki feel?

Do they hover under the city, alongside the sewer lines,
or in the scrappy trees left in the Park of Four Waters?
They must recognize the joy in our faces — to feel the rain,
to smell the air, the instant exhilaration.
Surely, they too set out vessels to catch the rain
beneath the edges of their homes. They used the rainwater for drinking,
cooking, mixing pottery clay, and for mixing paints.

The contrast is stark between the homes that existed hundreds
of years ago in this area and materials that "protect" them now.
The earthen covered canals, which were witnesses
to the ingenuity and success
of the Hohokamki, are now lined with cement.
The old gnarled trees also bear centuries of memories —
of disasters, of celebrations, of transitions of all types.

That the trees and the land survived is a wonder in itself.

Conversations at the Gila River Arts Center

The medicine man and I arrange to meet on a warm spring morning at the Gila River Arts Center restaurant south of Phoenix. The sky is bright blue and empty.

Over coffee, he began with this story.

• • •

There's a mountain north of here—you passed it driving here from Phoenix. We have always been told not to climb it, and we don't. It has tempting and dangerous slopes, and people who aren't from here can't resist climbing it. Once this guy was looking at it and asked, "You ever climb that?" "Nope," I said. "Too dangerous."

Actually, spirits live on that mountain, and some of our most sacred places are there. At certain times, the medicine people will make offerings or go to receive blessings atop the mountain. They're the only ones who are allowed to go there. The kids know this, and while they might not understand why it's forbidden, they know it's a place to be respected and even to be feared.

Anyway, this guy has to meet this challenge head-on. So he got ready and a couple of days later told me that he was going to hike up just so someone would know where he was. I wished him luck and warned him again that it wasn't a good idea. He smiled and left anyway. A few days later, I saw him at the cafe and he was on crutches. He had slipped before he reached the top and fractured his ankle. He was embarrassed, but I told him he wasn't the first person that that had happened to.

• • •

As our breakfast was brought to the table, he continued, "The Holy People take care of themselves. They do. Just as they take care of us. I really like those old stories and I always feel good when someone wants to hear them. It's good when someone wants to understand what we know and what we believe in. That's the Indian way all over—to sit and tell stories together. Each tribe is the same but the stories different. It's a good thing, this storytelling."

As we finished breakfast, the medicine man's daughter came in with her two small children. She teaches a class in traditional basket weaving and was surprised by the enrollment and the fact that so many women wanted to learn the old ways. As a child, she had asked to learn to weave, and her grandmother had gratefully taught her.

In preparation for the class, she had gathered the plants needed for the baskets and soaked them overnight in large metal tubs. She showed the women where the plants grew, as well as how and when they should be harvested. This morning a dozen or so students followed her across the patio to the classroom. Only two were non-Indians in the group of women who followed their instructor, this young Pima woman whose children ran after her, pouting, unwilling to share their mother.

After several more stories, as I left the Arts Center, two tourists came in, and across the highway at a small store, people talked and laughed. Some set up tables facing the road, preparing to sell jewelry, beadwork, tamales, and frybread. Huge jars of dill pickles and swivel racks of colored syrup for snow cones sat on the folding tables. Patio umbrellas were up— the sun was overhead and without trees nearby it was already hot. I pulled over and got out to see what they were selling.

"Bet you're Hopi," one guy said to me.

I smiled and said, "Navajo."

"Hey," he said, "I coulda started a war here!"

Everyone nearby laughed. Then I told them I was doing some writing for the city. A woman told me her son had married a Navajo woman, and they now lived in Santa Fe.

"It seems so far away," she said, "we hardly go up there. But at least they come back every once in a while."

"It is far," I agreed and talked about my parents in New Mexico and of how I worry about them.

"That's the way it is," she said, "but the elderly are a lot stronger than we think." We smiled.

I bought a frybread and a Diet Coke and started back to the car.

"Come back again. We're always here—selling and getting rich!" one woman said, laughing.

"Tell everyone at Hopi we said 'Hi,'" they teased me again.

As I drove back to Phoenix, the traffic was heavy and the air hot. Heat waves shimmered above the freeway. Off to the right were the huge plants used for basket making and the formidable mountain—a looming, dusky purple. In a few minutes, I was a part of the traffic rushing into the city. The roar of planes above pushed inside the car where the radio sang, and I drove on, alone except for my silent breathing.

Later in the day at the Pueblo Grande site, as I looked over the excavated area and at the huge cement pillars now installed there, I remembered the voices and the stories from earlier in the day. The construction crews had left the equipment parked in neat rows, and the ground beneath was dry brown, newly dug. The presence of pottery pieces, clothing fibers, bone shards—signs of former village life—were imperceptible.

Yet the Hohokamki had been there. As part of the arts team, I saw the small paper sacks of excavated remains standing upright in the bright sun.

All these centuries later, we stood in the center of their homes. I sat now under the trees in the heavy silence, still wanting to talk, to laugh, to share stories.

"We're all still here," I said to the Hohokamki whose homes were disturbed. "And we are still the same," I said. At that moment, it was obvious that there are memories and stories too powerful for things as new as cement and asphalt to destroy.

The worlds I had entered that morning were the prayers and hopes the Hohokamki had thrown ahead for all of us. It is the same now. We pray several times a day for ourselves, our ancestors, our children, and our grandchildren. The Kiowas call this "throwing our prayers"—we cast our prayers seven generations ahead. This destruction of the Hohokamki villages and the construction of the expressway embody this concept for many people.

Daané'é Diné

In the midst of Phoenix,
the warm March sun is overhead.
Traffic rushes by, and every ten minutes or so
airplanes lift off or glide onto the black runways.
A train slithers by, our voices quiver from the vibrating air.
The ground beneath us shivers.

We are witnesses to the excavation
of the old Hohokamki homes
where archaeologists are working
at the Pueblo Grande site.
A cache of clay animals was unearthed this afternoon,
and a ripple of excitement swept through the work site.
This is the most significant find to date.

The archaeologists feel certain that the small figures
are ritual ceremonial images. The figures were in the center
of a pithouse alongside a huge pot that had been shattered
by centuries of dirt and layers of civilization.

A small dog stood upright; its neck had been broken,
then reattached, evidenced by a small crack line.
There were other dogs, sheep, and some goats.
The miniature clay bodies were chubby,
the surfaces uneven and bumpy. The fingertips

of whoever had made them were clearly embedded.
These small figures stood upright as if the children
had just left and would be returning to continue their play.

At the end of the day, I returned to my hotel room, several hundred yards
from the site, and tried to push the images of little clay animals from my
mind. I ate, tasting nothing, and watched TV a bit. Then I lay down, closed
my eyes, and dreamt of my childhood.

On a clear, warm day we played under the huge cottonwoods surrounding
the house. My mother came out and sat down with us, spreading her skirt
out around her. "Shúúh, look, I'll show you how to make some toy people,"
she said, taking a small cloth square and putting a pile of sand in the center.
"Díígi 'át'éego ádeiilyaa, shiyázhí, like this, my little ones," she murmured,
turning the cloth-covered ball right-side-up, forming the head. Then she put
a stick into the center of the ball so that the remaining cloth formed a skirt,
and a small crosswise stick made the arms of a woman. "Jó áko," she said,
"daané'é asdzáán iilyaah. We have made a doll woman." We drew in her face
and daané'é asdzáán stood ready to play.

"K'ad hastiin sha'? How about making a toy man?" We tore more squares
of cloth, filled the centers with sand, tied them, and put in center sticks to
make them stand up. "There," my mother said. "K'ad iilyaah. We've made a
toy family." She got up, gathering her skirt, and went inside to make bread.
We looked at the little figures standing in the dirt—a mother, father, and five
children of varying sizes.

"Ti', shiáłchini," my sister said, pretend-talking to the dolls, "Chi'yáán
'ásdįįd. Naalghhéhé bá hooghangóó deekai. Let's go, my children. There is
no more food. We are going to the store." We put the people and some little
mud animals on a flat piece of wood and pushed the imaginary car to a
make-believe store under the next tree.

The next morning, the eastern sky glowed clean yellow. The sun had not yet risen. From the hotel window, I could see the Pueblo Grande site. Thin wisps of fire smoke rose from the camps of the homeless who stayed nearby. I wondered if they heard noises from the excavation site at night or if they saw the spirits of the Hohokamki, who were being unearthed, walking about. Maybe the wandering spirits of the Hohokamki gathered with the homeless, some of whom are recent war veterans and feel similarly displaced in modern America.

And I wondered what had happened to the toys we had made as children. Had they been absorbed back into the soft dirt beside my parents' house? Had they been carried off by the wind, or by our children? Had they been buried by seasons of rain, leaves, and snow?

Dust Precedes the Rain

"The water from the sink is no good for making pottery.
It just ruins it," my children's Acoma grandmother would say.
Thereafter, she sent the kids to replace the full bowls of rainwater
that had filled since it began to rain.
Her son said that when he was a child, the rain smelled
and tasted so good—he and other kids played outside,
laughing and running around—and they stopped once in a while to lick
the cool adobe walls. The sides of the smooth houses were
fragrant and nurturing. From atop the mesa at Acoma Pueblo,
it is possible to see almost seventy miles in each direction.

It is the same on the reservations surrounding Phoenix.
Long before the rains come, the gentle desert wind
carries the scent of rain, wild plants flutter anxiously,
and pets frolic, acting silly. To the west, the thunderheads
loom dark and full. Thin waves of dust precede the rain,
rolling tumbleweeds and bits of paper, and the children run and skip,
allowing the wind to push them along. They yell and laugh.
The lilting sounds are carried eastward by the blowing slants
of rain—their laughs and shouts caught in the leaves of sturdy trees.
They linger in the crevices of small hills and arroyos
and finally swirl into the slopes of the purple mountains nearby.

It must have been the same when the Hohokamki lived here
where the expressway crosses over. The children played

in the dust-charged breezes, shouting and running in circles,
and when the rains began, they paused, their faces turned upward
to taste the cool clean rain.

Their quiet gratitude for brimming pots of water remains
now in the crumbling re-buried walls of their small homes.
The still concentration with which they painted pottery
remains entwined in the roots of these huge old trees.
The exuberant spirits of the children remain too,
in the small toys and tiny woven sandals that were unearthed:
their spirits remain in the dry grains of dirt
that were dug up by shovels, backhoes, and bulldozers.

This is evident in the persistence of the bright wild plants
that push their way out of the dry ground.
This is evident in the new growth that springs up
along the arroyos and streams following sudden rains.
This is evident in the island of peaceful silence
that the museum cradles amid the city's frenzy.
This is evident in the restless energy of the busloads
of children who visit the old homes of the Hohokamki today.
They recognize the old history that is theirs.
They recognize the old history that is ours.

It Was

I won't return to the startling beauty of the valley
where stars glimmer bright. And so many.
I stood in the quiet road amazed.
It seemed a fantasy. It was.

The stars and dark steep mountains circle us.
Beneath the huge pines, deer wind a careful path
to the waiting water. They know no guilt.

Inside the circle of water, the clear rippling twin of moon,
coyote's careless handiwork of stars, the deep black sky
The water is still, quiet lapping at the edges.
Mosquitoes hum, waiting, waiting.
The water does not remember you and me
sharing stories, teasing, laughing at lunch.

Perhaps those afternoons' bright sounds linger
in the trees, the steep cliffs, the dry air.
But what good is memory if this place
does not recognize me? Or you?

Later, a low din dissipates into the floor of the valley.
Inside the glass-walled banquet rooms,
people are reading and talking poetry.
Wine glasses clink, sheaf of poems shuffles,

peals of laughter descend into the cool night.
I am there, reading words and smiling.
I am not there; I watch the wide back doors.
	I drive slowly past houses of fine aged wood
	and huge glazed windows.
	I know no songs to draw you out
	to the night's lingering beauty.

You are inside a huge, dark house,
a silent shelter of your own thoughts.
Everything you should have said echoes over and over.
You are drinking too much.

There is no symmetry here though the deer
are lying down now in the hushed mountainside.
There is no symmetry in the glorious disarray of distant stars.
There is no symmetry though stories are buried in the mountainside.
There is no symmetry though songs burn when glowing stars fall.

Tell me.
Tell me now.
What good are words that wither
in the clean, silver slants of moonlight?

Notes for the Children

1

Long ago the Holy Ones built the first hooghan for First Man and First Woman with much planning and deliberation; then they started in the east doorway, blessing the house for the protection and use of Navajo people. They moved clockwise from the east and offered prayers and songs in each direction. They taught us in hope that when we moved into a new apartment or home, we would do the same. They taught us this so that any unhealthy memories the house contained would leave; this was taught us so that the house would embrace us and recognize our gratitude. The Holy Ones knew that homes need prayers and songs, just as we do. To acknowledge a new home in this way ensures that the family will be nourished and protected. You can ask a medicine or clergy person to do this. And the Holy Ones appreciate it if you must perform this yourself. They understand English, too.

2

Once my father asked, "Have you ever seen your mother wear slacks?" I thought a moment, and with surprise I answered, "No." "In the old way," he said, " Asdzání " — "woman" — means the same thing as a skirt. This is why Diné women have always worn skirts. It's something to think about." I remember my mother spreading her skirt out in a half-circle when we were away from home so that we could nap, play or eat upon it, almost like a tablecloth. Her skirt was good to hide inside, and she had safety pins pinned in the folds "just in case." She used her skirt as a blanket, towel, and sometimes a wash cloth. They say that the round roof of a female hooghan is like a woman's flared skirt because the woman is the center of the Diné home. This is why an old blessing song says, "The beauty of my home extends from the woman. Beauty extends from the woman." My father said this years ago just before I was leaving to speak publicly. I rushed into the bedroom and changed into a traditional skirt.

3

Long ago people did not have English names. They had two names—a sacred name given at birth and one that non-family members used because everyone used kinship terms within the community. Thus we learned that it is important to address others by acknowledging their relationship each time we speak to them. By saying "my younger sister" or "my older brother," they are reminded that you love and respect them. This is particularly true for anyone older than yourself. Older people are always thankful when the young ones show respect for Diné culture. If you have several grandmothers, you can say "My grandma Sue" to distinguish one from the others. This teaching extends to school or college where it's better not to address a teacher, employer, or any other older person by their first name. One must remember that good manners last for centuries and centuries.

4

Diné people far from home are always scheming and planning as to how to get some mutton and Bluebird or Red Rose flour. When we hear of someone going back to the rez, we offer them money and ask humbly that they bring flour or mutton back for us. If car space is a problem, we say "Even just a bit of the backbone is okay." Mutton has long been a staple of Diné life and is a literal reminder of the many meals at home, celebrations and events of all types, fairs, and ceremonies. When we taste mutton, we are reminded of the mountains, the air, the laughter and humor surrounding a meal, but mostly we are reminded of loved ones. And everyone knows that only Bluebird or Red Rose flour will work for náneeskaadí and frybread. Some elderly people say that mutton has healing powers and brings happiness because sheep have been a part of our history since the beginning of time.

The last time I returned from home, I checked as luggage an ice cooler full of mutton, frozen chile, and dry ice, and the airline agent had to inspect the contents because of the recent terrorist activity. "What's in here?" she asked. "Mutton and chile," I replied. "Mutton?" she asked, puzzled. The chile she could understand since we were in Albuquerque. Her supervisor came over and said, "You have mutton in there?" "Yes," I said. "It's meat," clarifying things. "Hmm-m," he mused. Then I picked up a square of frozen mutton and let him inspect it. "We can't get this kind in Kansas," I explained. "Okay," he said. "Tape up the cooler and label it." To the delight of many in Kansas, I returned with mutton that we ate sparingly and only on special occasions. Others heard about it, so it was divided into smaller portions so that there would be enough for all who wanted some. I didn't try to bring a twenty-five pound bag of Bluebird flour because it would have been too heavy to lift into the plane's overhead storage, and it is simply too fragile to check as luggage.

Diné people are known to complain at times, "What kind of meal is this? There's no mutton stew!" So if you're far from home, remember there might be other Diné people around who are probably craving mutton. Bring some back for them, and they will probably tell stories as you eat. Later they will share with you when you really need it. This mutton business is a distinct Diné trait, and it will probably never change.

This Is How They Were Placed for Us

I

Hayoołkáałgo Sisnaajiní nihi neł'iih łeh.
Blanca Peak is adorned with white shell.
Blanca Peak is adorned with morning light.
She watches us rise at dawn.
Nidoohjeeh shá'áłchíní, nii leh.
Get up, my children, she says.

She is the brightness of spring.
She is Changing Woman returned.
By Sisnaajiní, we set our standards for living.
Bik'ehgo da'iiná.

Because of her, we think and create.
Because of her, we make songs.
Because of her, the designs appear as we weave.
Because of her, we tell stories and laugh.
We believe in old values and new ideas.
Hayoołkáałgo Sisnaajiní bik'ehgo hózhónígo naashá.

II

This is how they were placed for us.
Ałní' ní' áago Tsoo dził áníi łeh, "Da'oosá, shá'áłchíní."
In the midday sunlight, Mount Taylor tells us,
"It's time to eat, my little ones."

She is adorned with turquoise.
She is adorned with lakes that sparkle in the sunlight.
Jó 'éí biniinaa nihitah yá'áhoot'ééh.
Tsoo dził represents our adolescence.
Mount Taylor gave us turquoise to honor all men,
thus we wear turquoise to honor our brothers,
we wear turquoise to honor our sons,
we wear turquoise to honor our fathers.
Because of Tsoo dził, we do this.

We envision our goals as we gaze southward.
Each summer, we are reminded of our own strength.
T'áá hó' ájít' iigo t'éiya dajinii łeh.
Tsoo dził teaches us to believe in all ways of learning
Ałní' ní' áago Tsoodził bik'ehgo hózhónígo naashá.

III

This is how they were placed for us.
E'e'aahjigo, Dook'o'oosłííd sida.
To the west, the San Francisco Peaks are adorned with abalone.
Each evening she is majestic.
She is adorned with snow.
She is adorned with the white light of the moon.

The San Francisco Peaks represent the autumn of our lives.
Asdzání dahinilníí doo.
Dinééh dahinilníí doo.

In the autumn of our lives,
they will call us woman.
In the autumn of our lives,
they will call us man.

The San Francisco Peaks taught us to believe in strong families.
Dook'o'oosłííd binahji' danihidziił.
The San Francisco Peaks taught us to value our many relatives.
E'e'aahjígo Dook'o'oosłííd bik'ehgo hózhónígo naashá.

IV

This is how they were placed for us.
Chahałheełgo Dibé Nitsaa, "Da'ołwosh, shá'áłchíní," níi łeh.
From the north, darkness arrives—Hesperus Peak—
urges us to rest. "Go to sleep, my children," she says,
She is adorned with jet.
She is our renewal, our rejuvenation.
Dibé Nitsaa binahji' laanaa daniidzin łeh.
Hesperus Peak taught us to have hope for good things.

Haigo sáanii, dahinilníí doo.
Haigo hastóíí, dahinilníí doo.
In the winter of our life, they will call us elderly woman.
In the winter of our life, they will call us elderly man.
In the winter of our life, we will be appreciated.
In the winter of our life, we will rest.
Chahałheełgo Dibé Nitsaa bik'ehgo hózhónígo naashá.

This is how the world was placed for us.
In the midst of this land, Huerfano Mountain
is draped in precious fabrics.
Her clothes glitter and sway in the bright sunlight.
Gobernador Knob is clothed in sacred jewels.
She wears mornings of white shell.
She wears the midday light of turquoise.
She wears evenings of abalone, the light of the moon.
She wears nights of black jet.

This is how they were placed for us.
We dress as they have taught us,
adorned with precious jewels
and draped in soft fabrics.

All these were given to us to live by.
These mountains and the land keep us strong.
From them, and because of them, we prosper.

With this we speak,
with this we think,
with this we sing,
with this we pray.

This is where our prayers began.[3]

Above the Canyon Floor

The thin, hot air shimmered above the canyon floor. The sheep grazed quietly, their bells clinking. The faint echo drifted through the trees and into the crevices of the smooth red cliffs.

The sunset's dark pink and orange hues cast the entire canyon in streaks of long, slightly dusty, fading sunlight. Áshiih Neez noticed a young woman walking alongside the thin stream on the other side of the canyon. Her long hair glistened in the evening sunlight. He hadn't seen her before. He wondered where she could have come from. Áshiih Neez had grown up in the canyon, so he knew all the families in the area. From where he leaned back against tsé haadeesk'id, a huge pointed rock tucked underneath the sheer, steep walls, he knew she couldn't see him. Tsé haadeesk'id felt warm and smooth against his back in the rapidly cooling summer evening. In Canyon de Chelly, the summer days are hot and bright, yet once the sun sets, the temperature quickly drops almost forty degrees.

He slid off the huge rock and began to shoo the sheep homeward, shushing them and waving long willow branches. The dogs ran circles around the sheep, excited finally to have something to do. They liked herding and guarding the sheep, and occasionally they circled around for words of approval from Áshiih Neez. He followed the animals, whistling and singing to himself.

As they turned the curve by Kin naałdaas, sliding house, the young woman suddenly stepped out of a grove of small trees. He was startled momentarily. "Yá'át'ééh," she said. "Hooghangóósh díníyá? Are you returning to your home?" she asked. "I saw you back there lying on the

rock." "Yes," he said, "I was watching you." Áshiih Neez noticed her deli-
cate features; slender and smooth hands , dark bronze skin, and she wore
thin long jaatłóół—earrings of fine turquoise tipped with white shell and
two small necklaces of turquoise and coral.

She fell in step beside him and they walked quietly, occasionally glanc-
ing at one another and smiling. Áshiih Neez was astounded by her beauty,
yet embarrassed because he felt so plain beside her. Then he suddenly real-
ized he hadn't asked her about her clans. "Ha'át'íísh dóone'é nílí?" he asked,
partly dreading her answer because if one of her four primary clans was
the same as his, they would be related. He would have to leave immedi-
ately. Smiling, she named not only her four clans but also her grandparents
three and four generations back. He was impressed. She was so young to
have such detailed knowledge. They both laughed a little with relief when
it was clear they weren't related. "I was afraid," she said smiling.

They walked behind the sheep, and as they talked they fell further back.
After a while, she stopped and sat down alongside the stream. "My feet
are hot," she said, and she removed her moccasins and put her feet into the
cold, clear stream. Áshiih Neez knelt beside her and watched the dogs herd
the sheep homeward. "The dogs are trained well," he said. "They'll get the
sheep back by themselves."

By now the sun had set, and darkness moved into the canyon; the huge
walls cast long, cold shadows across its floor. Above the top of the canyon,
the pale light of the rising moon flickered over the desert brush and small
piñon trees. She walked backwards slowly, facing him as she told about
how the Utes had attacked the Navajos long ago in the nearby canyon.
Áshiih Neez asked her open-ended questions so that he could listen to her.

Finally, they sat down on a flat, round boulder that still radiated the
sun's warmth. He leaned back and lay down, looking at the dark sky over-
head. From the bottom where they were, the sky was a rectangle of stars,

moonlight, and black space. Nearby a small animal moved in the shrubs, cracking branches and rustling dry leaves. As he held her, he thought of summer rain—the clear, sweet scent of sage and wet earth. During the night she hummed or sang songs that are sung during the long summer nights at a healing ceremony. One song told of calling a handsome man who was at the fires that are kept burning. During the ritual, while the patient prayed and was being prayed over, at a distance from the main ceremonial structure, the young people glanced at one other and joined in singing humorous and flirtatious songs. They smiled at each other across the huge fire and from behind the circle of singers.

Áshiih Neez and the young woman held each other, the rock's warmth beneath them, her full cotton skirt covering them, and her hair loose—a dark circle fragrant with the day's sunlight and the canyon air. When he laughed, the sound echoed and bounced off the steep walls and drifted into the trees bordering the trails and thin, cold streams. "I'll take you home," Áshiih Neez murmured. "Then we will live near your mother. It will all be good." She nodded and fell asleep. He slept soundly all night.

He was startled awake by the chirping and noisy conversation of birds. Somewhere nearby dogs were barking, chasing sheep out for the day. All the noises were amplified by the echoing in the canyons. Áshiih Neez was alone. He glanced about frantically and realized he was in an entirely different place. He woke on the same flat rock, but nothing else existed as before. His heart pounded with fear as he saw that there was only empty space all around him. Far off in the distance, he saw the familiar canyon walls, but now he was above them. The stream they walked beside was far below—thin and shiny with water. The rock had risen almost seven hundred feet on a tall sandstone spiral during the night. "How could this happen?" Áshiih Neez wondered aloud. His mind raced. Where could she have gone? Now it dawned on him that he didn't even know her name.

He was overwhelmed with fear and loss. In the bright morning light, he leaned and looked over the edge of the rock. There was no way to get down. The rock itself perched like a flat saucer on top of the narrow spiral. Its sides were smooth, carved stone. He sat trying to think and plan, and then he launched into a long, rambling prayer, pleading for help and his life.

Then far below, Áshiih Neez saw an elderly woman walking near the base of the rock. Surely she'll notice that this rock wasn't here yesterday, he thought. But the woman kept her head bowed; her back was stooped from age. "Shimásána, my grandmother," he yelled down to her. "Try to get help for me." His voice echoed loudly through the canyon. It seemed as if she hadn't heard him. He yelled out again, "Help me, my mother!" Still she continued walking. He became desperate and shouted, "Hey! Help me. I need help to get down. Please." This time she stopped. He called out once again for help and then she turned and looked directly at him. She squinted and brushed long strands of white hair from her brow. "Áłtsé. Wait," she said.

Relief swept over Áshiih Neez. He felt sure he would be rescued. When I get down, he thought, I'll find the one who is to be my wife. Meanwhile, the old woman walked to the base of the towering rock and out of Áshiih Neez's sight. He had confidence in the woman, and he waited for her instructions. After a while, she called to him, "I am weaving a rope for you to use. Be patient as it will take some time to cover the long distance." Her voice sounded oddly familiar, but he pushed the thought aside and whispered prayers of gratitude for her help. He was surprised that she was weaving, because at the time only Pueblo people wove. Maybe she had once been a captive of the Pueblos, he surmised.

By mid-morning, the top of the rope reached Áshiih Neez. The old woman showed him how to climb by balancing his feet on the smooth sides of the pinnacle. He followed her, inching downward on tightly woven wool rope. The rope was thick and pliable. She reached the ground ahead of him and waited in the cool shade of small piñon trees.

As soon as Áshiih Neez descended, he looked about for the woman he was to marry. Perhaps she had come back, he thought. As he approached the elderly woman to thank her, she looked downward, as is customary, and shook hands with him. "Thank you," he said. "You have truly helped me. I could have died up there."

She remained silent, and then he noticed that her earrings and necklaces were exactly the same as those of his wife-to-be. He stared at her jewelry in surprise, then became embarrassed by his rudeness. "I am the one you are looking for," she said. Áshiih Neez recognized her voice, and he looked into her face as if he could see the young woman within. As he stood there, he was overcome with sadness. It became clear that indeed this was the one who sang into the night for him. He knew the warm smoothness of her skin; he remembered her even breathing as she slept.

Áshiih Neez had heard stories of such women. It was true that he had met her—she who could change herself from a young, strong woman to one who was elderly, knowledgeable, and caring. Áshiih Neez had been with her, a powerful and wise being. His eyes shone with tears and sadness. He knew that they would not have a life together.

"Áshiih Neez," she said, "you are a kind and tender man, but I am not an earth surface person. I am called Spider Woman. I am here to help the people. When you marry," she said, "let your little girls herd sheep near here. I will be here, and I will teach them to weave. With this skill, your family will prosper. Because of weaving, the Navajos will never be destitute. Only the women will weave, Áshiih Neez. They will provide for their families along with the men."

She touched his arm and walked into a small stone house at the base of the towering rock. The stones were intricately linked and perfectly placed, appearing to be even, flat stone and woven together. There was no mud or plaster filling.

Áshiih Neez walked home slowly in the bright midday light. The woman's touch still tingled on his arm, and he was immersed in sadness. Then he heard his dogs panting, and sure enough, as he turned the corner, his sheep were moving westward down the canyon. He laughed a little and sighed at such an ordinary sight.

It is said that here, at the base of Spider Rock, weaving was given to Navajo women, beginning with Áshiih Neez's daughters. The little girls were astute learners and began the tradition of rug weaving. It is Spider Woman who said that Navajo women should have a skill to help provide for their families. "Just because a man wants to marry you doesn't mean he's going to take care of you forever," she said.

The Ground Is Always Damp

One night Leona dreamt that she was sitting outside her parents' home in the bright sunlight. The many trees, the small dusty chickens scratching nearby, and a single cloud above cast sharp dark shadows on the smooth yard. The sudden familiarity of the detailed shadows and clean air startled and awakened her, and later she spoke aloud, addressing her mother who was hundreds of miles away.

"Shimá, my mother, it's cloudy here most of the time. The ground is always damp, and Mom, I don't care to kneel down and sift dirt through my fingers. One day last week, the sun came out for a few hours, and the shadows were soft and furry on the brown grass. That's the way it is here, my mother."

Even though Leona hadn't seen her parents in months, she talked to them silently every day. She imagined that they listened, then responded by explaining things or asking long, detailed questions. Leona did this thoughtfully and felt that they did the same in their daily conversations about her and her children. They wondered what the weather was like and what kind of house Leona and her family lived in. She was certain about this. The difference was that they spoke aloud to each other, or to the various brothers and sisters who lived nearby.

In her dreams, she was always there in New Mexico, driving the winding roads to Taos, watching the harvest dances at Laguna, or maybe selling hay and watermelons with her brothers. In her dreams, she laughed, talking and joking easily in Navajo and English. She woke herself up sometimes because she had laughed aloud, or said, "Aye-e-e"—that old familiar teasing expression.

The New Mexico sky is clear and empty. It is a deep blue, almost turquoise, and Leona's family lives surrounded by the Carriso Mountains in the west, the Sleeping Ute Mountains in the north, the La Plata in the east and the Chuska Mountain range to the southwest. They rely on the distance, the thin, clean air, and the mountains to alert them to rain, thunderstorms, dust storms, and intense heat. At various times, her brothers stand looking across the horizon to see what is in store. They can see fifty miles or more in each direction.

In contrast, when Leona looks to the east most mornings, the sky is gray, the air thick with frost, and the wind blows cold dampness.

"My mother, there are no mountains here, and I can't see very far because the air is thick and heavy with a scent I can't recognize. I haven't been able to smell the arrival of snow here, or to distinguish between the different kinds of rain scent. The rain seems all the same here, except in degree, and it is constant. Sometimes it lasts for two days and nights. It pours steadily until brown streams form and drain into the overflowing creek behind the house.

"Shimá, some nights I just want to walk down the street and smell piñon wood smoke, or stew or beans boiling when I pass a house." In the fall, we talk about the seasonal rituals at home. "Remember," we say, "fresh green chile roasting outside at Farmer's Market or outside of Smith's or Albertson's? When Grandma Acoma baked bread in the outside oven at McCarty's? We all helped. Daddy chopped wood and piled it near the oven. We helped put the oven door back in place and ran out of the house with potholders and the long poles to bring out the bread. We would help Grandma carry the bread, and she would say, 'Chase the dogs off! They just get in the way!'"

Once Leona's elder daughter said, "Then we didn't know that those times would be memories for us. We didn't know we would leave there. It seemed like it would last and last. The bright afternoons, Grandma's soft strong hands, the smell of bread in the clear blue sky."

"Our laughter was different then," she said softly.

No Denials from Him

It was music, after all, that saved me, I suppose. Songs on the radio, songs in restaurants and in stores; their rhythmic pleas and stories soothed me. They soothed the person I had become: the one he left for someone else, the one he no longer loved.

One night, I was sleeping alone at the very edge of the bed when I dreamt he was with a woman, holding her and speaking softly to her. The shock of it—his loving her—pushed me onto the floor. I awoke stunned, sobbing. I knew then that he would leave me. I needed no proof, no denials from him. I believe my dreams.

After that it was a matter of time. On Friday nights as he drove those long, barren miles home, did he wonder how to tell me? Or did he smile, remembering her? Monument Valley is the perfect name for that huge place. At night the mesas cast black shadows for miles. He drove through those spaces, swollen with such beauty, and the moon so clear and round. Maybe he felt content then. As he drove home those nights, his foot resting on the gas pedal, country music swirling in the truck cab, did he rest his arm on the window frame?

Tell me, I would like to ask him, what was it like to drive home to us after that? We were nestled here, among pine trees, in these low mountains surrounding our home. The baby slept, I mixed bread dough, the two little ones argued about which TV show to watch. Our twelve-year-old brooded in her room and listened to music banging through headphones. I watched the time and rushed to have supper ready when you drove in. "Just wash your hands and sit down here," I thought I would say. "You must be tired." Outside spring winds blew through the trees, and pine branches brushed against the house and touched the window panes lightly. I listened to the wind as I made náneeskaadí, slapping the warm dough back and forth and shaping it into almost perfect circles. The grill was hot, warming evenly, and the smell of bread filled the kitchen. When I was a child, the sounds of my mother making bread comforted me.

Now as the woman whom you left, the thought of making bread, so easily, so calmly—an act that meant I loved you, that meant you loved me, that meant our children were normal and happy—that single act called forth memories of my mother. Now, the thought of making náneeskaadí angers me. I told the children, "Someday, shá'áłchíní, my children, when things are better, I'll make a big stack of bread for all of you." What is it like for you? What does she cook for you? I have heard that Hopis don't make náneeskaadí. If that's true, can a Navajo man live not having something he was raised on?

Then he left and moved into her small house on the south side of the village. I imagined her home to be smooth and brown, with a wooden screen door and a sunken flat roof. I've heard that the wind blows so hard there that sand-drifts form around the windows and under the doors.

I felt as though I'd lost myself; as if the one who had been married for sixteen years was someone else. My days and nights became a blur of routine things—school, work, paying bills, buying groceries—all performed inside a vacuum of tears, anger, and exhaustion. It was no use to wear makeup; my eyelids stayed swollen and red. Sometimes it seemed that people couldn't hear me speak or that they were talking to me from far away. Their voices were thin and meaningless. "Speak louder," I wanted to say. "I can hardly understand you." Then I saw myself as he must have—short, fuzzy hair that tried to look upbeat, my weight not proportionate to my height. I noticed I had a tendency to slouch. "No wonder," I thought many times as I surveyed myself in department store mirrors or at cosmetic counters. "No wonder he's with a slim Hopi woman."

True, I had the kids and my teaching to consider the whole time. I told myself over and over that just because one's life falls apart doesn't mean classes can be canceled or that the children can be turned over to the human services department. I began to listen to the radio all the time; in my office, on the way to pick up the kids at school or soccer, on the way to the grocery store or to my brother's house. I slept with the radio on low all night and bought a fancy coffee maker that had a radio and turned itself on, so that in the morning I imagined that I wasn't really alone. When I first walked into the kitchen, it was as if someone had already made coffee and was talking or singing. Such things I did when there was hardly enough money to pay the utility bills.

Soon the school year was over and summer arrived. I felt relieved to leave Durango the kids and I went back to Black Mesa to stay at my parents' old summer place. My aunt and uncle were glad to see us and to have extra help with the sheep and other chores. It was so quiet there. The kids quickly found things outside to keep them occupied as there isn't electricity atop Black Mesa. At first they whined and complained—no TV, no Nintendo, no friends. Soon they adjusted and I saw them only at mealtimes or when one of them came in for a nap during the afternoon. I could get only KTNN on the radio and so that was on all the time. The sound of Navajo voices and country music felt just right.

The nights were so clear and quiet. Sometimes we spread a blanket on the ground and watched the stars. My uncle knew stories about various constellations, and when he came over, the kids listened quietly. Once in a while, I had to translate words into English for them.

Everything that had happened that spring seemed worlds away on those clear summer nights at Black Mesa. One day I made frybread for my aunt, and then the next day at our own place, I made náneeskaadí for my kids. I felt as if I had returned here to reclaim my life.

Slowly, with the radio on all the time, with the quiet still nights at Black Mesa, my kids shouting and laughing around me, and my aunt and uncle's house just a few hundred yards away, I came back. Yes, I was still overweight, but my perm had grown out, and I began to wear makeup again.

For some reason, all those songs about people being lonely, people being left, people yearning for someone absent, all those songs healed me. Why would songs like that exist if these things had never happened? I asked myself. Somewhere someone experienced these things and for some reason, either they, or someone else, wrote about it, then put music to the pain they felt.

They put music to the pain I thought was my death. They put music to the new life he gave me.

I Remembered This One in Tucson

When I lived in Albuquerque, I was going to my part-time job at the bookstore across from the university campus one afternoon. My friend Nita offered to drop me off on her way home. I didn't know she meant that literally.

She had just bought a new used convertible and was so excited when she was able to purchase it. She had had her eye on it for months and had even lit candles at church, hoping she could get it. Nita and I were good friends. We had both married young and had our older children about the same time, both life-changing events occurring in quick succession. For years, we both struggled to attend classes, pay day-care bills, and dress our kids and ourselves decently. So money was one thing there was never enough of. Anyway, it felt good when Nita finally saved enough money to buy the car she really wanted, the one she had dreamt about—neither an affordable little compact that got great mileage nor a sturdy car her parents gave her when they bought a larger luxury car.

True, it was a used car, but Kharmann-Ghias weren't made anymore. "A classic," we kept saying to each other. It was beautiful, a shiny orange body and creamy leather top. The price was good, and at the time we didn't consider the condition of the engine and that sort of thing. We went to the car lot during breaks between classes and simply looked at the car. We ran our hands over the leather interior and imagined driving up the winding roads to Sandia Crest with the top down. "Do you think I should?" she asked me a hundred times when she finally had the total amount. "Of course, you deserve it," I said, "not to mention I deserve to have a friend with a convertible." We decided not to tell our husbands because we wanted to surprise them. We felt sure they would be happy and proud.

After she bought it, the car drove like a dream (her words). I followed her back to campus, and nothing out of the ordinary happened. It drove well that evening when her family saw it for the first time. Her husband wasn't exactly ecstatic. Instead, he said things like, "You mean you just paid the sticker price? Did you try offering less?" "How could I?" Nita said. "That's the price it said, so that's what I paid." Over the years, we've become smarter in these matters.

Beginning the next week, the car became unpredictable. Nita drove the car half-time, and the rest of the time it was in an auto mechanic's garage. We found out quickly that a classic car's repair bills hovered near heaven somewhere. I lent Nita some money, but my husband said it wasn't our responsibility. "But I was there the whole time," I said. "I told her she deserved a car like that." "She does," he said. So we had yard sales and sold whatever we found in the remote corners of our homes at the flea market. I couldn't believe how expensive the repairs were. But we kept telling each other that after the brakes were done, it would be a long time before they'd go out again. But after the brakes were replaced, the transmission needed work. It seemed like it would never end. The insurance was high, too. Nevertheless, we remained optimistic that come summer we'd be cruising the Duke City and Santa Fe in the cute orange convertible, our kids tucked in the back seat.

The afternoon when Nita offered me the ride to the bookstore, I got in and it was so cool. The top was down and it was a bright spring day. I leaned back and looked at the turquoise sky as Nita was talking. Then in the middle of everything, she said, "Oh, I meant to tell you that once this car starts, I can't stop it. If I stop, it won't start again."

"What?" I murmured, trying to comprehend what this meant.

"Oh, it's really no problem," she said. "I'll drop you off in the alley behind the store rather than on Central." She paused. "I already thought this through. No problem."

"Okay," she continued, "I'll slow down real slow so that you can just get out. I've practiced this. I'll drive so slow that it'll seem like I'm stopped, but of course I won't be."

"Well, okay," I said. I could see that there was no other way. Besides, I needed to get to work.

We drove through the alley, and Nita told me to throw my shoes and purse out first. "They might weigh you down when you jump," she said. She drove as slowly as she could to show me how simple it would be just to jump out the next time through. After I threw my things out, we turned around in an empty parking lot and came back down, and just before the car was almost stopped, near the bookstore, for some reason I started screaming, "Now? now?"

"Go ahead!" Nita yelled.

"I can't! Eiyah!" I screamed.

"You have to! You have to!" she yelled, her voice rising with panic. Then just before I jumped, she accidentally hit the horn several times. We were both yelling and screaming as I landed on my hands and knees in the gravel right beside my purse. It happened so slowly, I even closed the door as I was leaping out. Then suddenly it was quiet, and Nita sped off, raising a bit of dust and waving. "We did it!" she yelled. I got up and brushed myself off. Then I realized that several people had gathered in the alley to investigate the noises. I was so embarrassed, yet I managed to walk away with one or two shreds of dignity. Later, they said that people thought that we were being attacked in the alley.

"Oh no," I said. "Her car wouldn't stop, so I had to jump out when it was still moving."

I could tell that they just didn't understand.

White Bead Girl

FURIOUS VERSIONS, PART 6

The night grows
miscellaneous in the sound of trees.

But I own a human story,
whose very telling
remarks loss.
The characters survive through the telling,
the teller survives
by his telling; by his voice
brinking silence does he survive.
But, no one
can tell without cease
our human
story, and so we
lose, lose.

Yet, behind the sound
of trees is another
sound. Sometimes, lying
awake, or standing
like this in the yard, I hear it. It
ties our human telling
to its course
by momentum, and ours
is merely part
of its unbroken

stream, the human
and other simultaneously
told. The past
doesn't fall away, the past
joins the greater
telling, and is.

This morning the sun shines bright, yet it is very cold. Around here, we are always so happy when the sun comes out; it is such a nice change from the usual gray dreariness. Cold, sunny days like this make me want to bake yeast bread. My children and husband are always so surprised and happy. They sit down in the kitchen and begin eating the warm rolls with butter so that sometimes the bread doesn't even last until suppertime. The warm, nurturing scent lingers until early morning. Before I fall asleep at night, I give thanks that such little things bring gratitude and happiness to my family.

I am remembering times such as these, and tears well up in my aching eyes. This morning my daughter has run away. She left footprints—deep, small holes in the snow. The morning light casts shiny, translucent blue shadows around each step. From where I stand at the door, I cannot see the dark frozen bottoms of her steps. I stare at these prints as if they can tell me something, as if they had absorbed what she was thinking, as if they held her intentions, as if they contained her anger. The snow and the sun are so bright, my eyes begin to hurt. She's just fourteen, I say aloud several times. She's just fourteen. The cat rubs against my ankle and sits down to watch the snow with me.

It wasn't so many years ago that, on a bright spring afternoon, I called the doctor and found that my test results were positive. I drove right to my husband's office, smiling and laughing a bit, and he held me close, swirling me in a little circle. We told the children, Natalie and Sonny. Although they were happy, we saw the little wave of uncertainty that swept over Natalie's face—she is the younger of the two. After dinner, while we picked cherries in the backyard, we talked about all the things she would need to help teach the new baby. The baby would have to learn about so much more than just sleeping and drinking milk. That weekend we drove to my in-laws' home at the pueblo so that they could advise us and say prayers for a safe and healthy pregnancy. According to Navajo custom, our children address their paternal grandparents as "Nálí man" or "Nálí asdzáán." Upon our arrival, the children immediately shifted into "our Nálí Grandma and Nálí Grandpa love us more than you do" mode. In other words, they virtually ignored us. They trailed their grandpa everywhere he went, holding onto his hand or his belt loop. They liked to help Grandma fix meals, and when everyone sat to watch the news, Sonny rested his head on Grandma's lap while she stroked his hair and back. Natalie squeezed in beside Grandpa on the chair and pulled at his mustache. He would smile and say, "You're getting too chubby to sit by me. Pretty soon you'll have to sit in your own chair." "No, my Nálí, I'll always sit by you," she would murmur.

Early the next morning, we awoke the children and all of us went out, wrapped in blankets against the cool spring dawn. Grandma led us about a quarter mile to the east, and there we stood in a semicircle while Grandpa sang for the new baby. I didn't understand the words, but I remember the clear rays of dawn light streaming over the horizon; the children's sleepy, solemn faces; my children's father's face as he looked into the distance, listening to songs—the deep, clear rhythm rising and falling in the quiet air. Then Grandma prayed, and as she did, she made a small leather bundle of various objects—a bit of turquoise for a boy, a piece of white shell for a girl, a perfectly round piece of jet, grains of cornmeal, and other symbols of a good life. She and Grandpa fastened this with soft, delicate feathers and tied it to a cluster of sagebrush; then together they prayed for all of us—our young family, their old age, and the new life that the family welcomed. Grandma told the children, "You can play nearby, but remember to be careful near here, because this prayer feather is for your new baby, and only the wind can take it. Can you remember that? Don't untie it or play with prayer feathers. Remember this is for your baby." The children nodded as they watched a small breeze rustle the cluster of feathers. The children and I followed Grandma back to the house along the winding path through the small desert brush and bushes. The men came behind, talking in low voices. I hurriedly made tortillas when we got to the house. We ate a hot breakfast of potatoes, eggs, bacon, and fresh red chile. Grandpa teased me, saying, "One good thing about Navajos is that they sure make good tortillas." We all laughed. The sun was now completely up, and as it streamed in through the south window, we sat in the kitchen, the scent of hot coffee lingering and the children settling down, getting ready to go back to sleep. Grandpa picked Natalie up and carried her into the bedroom, even though she was too tall to be carried around. "I'm not a baby," Sonny announced, and he went to lie on the couch.

This is what I remember so clearly as I sit in the living room staring at my daughter's footprints in the snow. The memory appears so clear, so distinct though I hadn't thought of it in years. One night my father was telling stories and he said suddenly, as if it had just occurred to him, "This thing called memory is like nothing else. Once you remember something, it never leaves you. It's how we know that we have lived." Maybe this sudden clarity of memory I feel now is what he meant. Or maybe he sensed instinctively that I would one day be sitting alone on a winter morning, bewildered by the angry tracks of my sullen daughter. It's so cold now. Last night the temperature dropped below freezing. Where could she have gone? I didn't hear her leave. Before I went to bed, I peeked into her room and said, "Good night, baby." "Night, mom," she said, sitting cross-legged on the floor, surrounded by papers and books. I didn't notice what she was wearing. The officer asked me this morning, "Can you tell us what she was wearing?" I couldn't. How stupid, I thought. What kind of mother doesn't even know how her kid is dressed? How else would they know her? She has long hair, a quick smile, and she is slender and pretty. How many other runaways look like her? How will they know her? I looked at all her clothes in her room, and so help me, I still couldn't tell what was missing. Though I'm certain that she is wearing jeans. What a breakthrough.

When she was born, I thought the labor would never end. My parents rushed from their home some three hundred miles away to be with us and to take care of the children. My father was nervous on the drive over because he thought they would arrive too late for him to bless us and to sing the birth songs. Daddy didn't normally advocate speeding, but my brother said he kept repeating, "Tsxííł niinti—Try to drive faster," every few miles. My brother thought it was funny. Various family members were planning to come into town on the weekend, and so there was intense excitement surrounding the birth. The doctors let my father pray over us— I was barely awake. When I went into the delivery room, I had some corn pollen dabbed on my forehead, and some more placed in a small pouch necklace around my neck. My mother was murmuring and encouraging me the whole time. When my daughter was born, my mother dotted the top of her head with pollen. The hospital was surprisingly willing to allow us to do all of these things. I fell asleep immediately, and when they brought my baby to me, she nursed loudly and her dark eyes flickered open every few minutes. We watched her, laughing, and were amazed at how she looked like all of us rather than just like her father or me. Her hair was thick and jet black. It stood up like the soft tufts on a feather.

On her fourth day, my parents presented her to the sun, our father, and named her "At'ééd Abíní" in memory of the early winter morning that welcomed her. Her name means the billows of morning mist that fill the valley above the winding river. Her name means woman of the morning—the first spark of creativity, the first ray of sunlight, the last glimmer of the white moon before it melts in the west. Her name means the world waited for her then rejoiced, as we did at her birth. Later that month, we took her to her nalis, her father's parents, and they, too, had a naming for her. The prayer bundle was tied with bright-colored string, and as we walked away we could see it, brilliant against the gray brush. Her name at her father's village is ceremonial and is called aloud when the katzinas and the sacred clowns present to her and the other children baskets of fruit, nuts, sweet treats, and pottery. Various katzinas call her several times a year and reward her for being thoughtful, kind, helpful at home, and successful in school. She walks out shyly to the center of the plaza and nods thank you as the whole pueblo watches. When the dancers call her, it is to remind us all of the happiness she brings to the family. These are her names—my slender daughter who now is in a place I am afraid to imagine. My daughter, it is so cold this morning. I think that the bright morning sun recalls naming her years ago. Watch over her, I whisper.

When she started school, we were worried because she had a set afternoon routine. We thought she wouldn't adjust. After lunch, she always watched *Little Rascals,* then took her nap with Floppy, her stuffed dog, Beatrice, her Cabbage Patch doll, and the blanket my mother made for her. But her brother and sister were at the same small school, so she wouldn't be alone. Her father and I sprinkled corn pollen around the windows and door and along the walls of her classroom. Her teacher, a young Hispanic man, prayed with us. We did this all together, though neither set of grandparents were with us. We prepared to let her go. Even though we had performed this blessing for the other two children too, it was harder for us this time. It's true that the youngest child is the most difficult to let go. We worried so. Yet she didn't cry when we left as the other kids had, and she continued to watch *Little Rascals* before nap time. She liked learning new things and seeing her brother and sister during the day. Once her nali grandma came to see the school's Christmas program. My daughter was dressed in red. She and three other children sang songs and played the piccolo. She seemed so serious and intense but not at all nervous. That evening, she and Grandma sang Christmas songs as we drove the seventy miles back to the pueblo. She wanted Grandma to hear all the songs she had learned. Even though it was dark in the car, I knew her father and Grandma were smiling at her enthusiasm and excitement. When we arrived at Grandma's home, she sang again for her Grandpa, who smiled and listened as he held her on his lap. "This Christmas Eve, baby," he said, "you have to lead the Christmas carols, because you sing better than all of us." "Okay," she said seriously, intently considering her new responsibility. On Christmas Eve when we returned from midnight mass, she led the singing for three songs, then fell asleep when the adults went to refill their coffee cups. Her sister said, "The little elf can't stay awake for Santa." Then Grandpa Nali said, "This old elf can't stay awake either, and I don't care about Santa." We all laughed, except for Natalie who said, "Grandpa, Santa might not come if you say that." But Santa did come.

That Christmas was not so long ago, and this morning I am wondering if there is something I failed to notice between those times of her childhood and now. Was there a sign I missed? Did I turn away from signs that would have told me she would walk quietly out the in the middle of a winter night? It seems that I should have been able to sense this. Why did I close the bedroom door last night? And why didn't the neighbor's dog bark? It was always barking at little things—squirrels and rabbits. What was I dreaming when she left? What kind of mother sleeps when her child is trudging through deep snow away from her? I stand here and look up into the pale blue sky. The sun is diffused. The bright morning light has faded into the afternoon. "Tell me what to do," I say. "Tell me what to do." Should I drive around town and look for her? But I should be here if the police call. Maybe she will come home. My baby, have you eaten today?

Hundreds of miles from here, at my mother's home, Mom and Daddy sit at the kitchen table drinking coffee. My mother clasps and unclasps her hands, and Daddy pats her arm. "She'll be okay," he says. "She'll be home soon." Since I called, they have offered prayers for her return several times. My mother said, "I couldn't sleep last night. I told your father, 'I hope everything's okay with our children.'" I cried and listened to my mother. They have grown so much older and are unable to travel as they used to. But at least we have phones now. My mother told me, "Your children will do things you don't understand. Sometimes they will bring you the worst grief you can ever feel. Yet because they are your children, you will forget the pain almost immediately when things are restored. Years from now, you will think that this was such a difficult time and you will remember what happened, but the pain will not be the same. Because each time they hug you after that, each time they serve you food, each time they laugh out loud with you, a bit of the pain leaves until only the outline of it remains and that alone becomes the memory." "Thank you, my mother," I said.

I sat on my daughter's bed several times today trying to look for clues. I looked for all the tell-tale signs of drug use—cigarette butts, lighters, beer cans, anything. Everything looked normal. I glanced through her collection of cassettes and CDs. What should I know about this music? What do these bands promote? Oh look, here's Mozart and Carlos Nakai. Are they signs of hope? Her brother has called several times and wants to begin the five-hour drive home from the university. "Just wait a while, son," I say. "She may come home tonight." "Mom, just remember, it's not your fault," he says, his voice tight and low. I say nothing, because I don't believe it. All I can think of is how I have become so disconnected from the world. Did I ever make my parents feel like this? In the end, I press her clothes against my cheek, smell her scent, and pray for all of us.

Last summer, she went on a trip with a group from school, and before she left we arranged to have a Hózhóójí, a blessing ceremony, for her. The medicine man spoke English, so he spoke to her in a mixture of Navajo and English. That morning she wore the outfit I made for the occasion. The blouse was black and bordered with small blue flowers, and the skirt was flared and solid black. I fixed her hair in the traditional way, tied with hand-spun wool, and she wore long turquoise earrings, two of her grandmother's necklaces, and a silver concho belt. Her collar clips sparkled in the sun. My sister said she looked like nihinálí asdzáán, our father's mother. The medicine man explained the ceremony to her, saying that long ago the holy people had made these songs and prayers for their children who would have to leave their homes, or who would leave the Navajo country. "This is how the holy people know us," he said, "by the songs and prayers they gave us. They'll say, 'Look, there is a Navajo away from her people. We can tell that person is a Navajo.'" He showed her the sacred stones and the ears of corn. "This," he said, "represents Changing Woman. This represents you. It shows us that young girls like yourself are strong because you're Navajo. You have extra help, too, because of your Pueblo side," he said. Outside, he handed her the basket and instructed her to lift it four times—to the east, to the south, to the west, and to the north. She repeated prayers after him and he sang for us. Her father and I stood nearby listening. The ceremony lasted most of the day, and when it ended she carried pollen to everyone in the room so that they could offer their prayers as well. As she carried the basket around the room, the medicine man said to her, "You're a different person now. You're not the same girl you were yesterday. Now you have the blessings and strength of the holy people. Thank you," he said, "for having this ceremony, because now we have all been strengthened along with you. Thank you." We were all happy about the ceremony and had a big meal afterwards. It was good to be with the whole family again. It was good for the children to see ceremonies such as this. My daughter's trip went well, and she kept a bit of pollen tucked in her wallet. Her sister, Natalie, gave her a small ring saying, "Grandpa said Navajos always wear turquoise." She wore the ring.

Now as evening light falls, I wonder if my daughter remembers this, if she is wearing the turquoise ring. I am fairly certain she is without pollen. As the night's darkness folds in from the north, I can do no more than this — pray, remember, pray, review her life, review our lives, pray. Then I remember a little song she liked and I sing it for my daughter, wherever she may be.

At 3:15 the next morning the phone rings. The police have found my daughter. I can hardly speak as we rush to retrieve her. There she is — turned from us, her hair disheveled and clothes wrinkled. Quickly I memorize what she's wearing. I walk up behind her and touch her. I am literally shaking. She turns and bursts into tears. My daughter has returned. Her face is sad, yet I can only hope she knows the meanings of her name, of all her ceremonies, and of her own searching heart.

As we arrive home, she and Natalie retreat to her room to talk. Natalie holds her as if she will disappear again. I call her brother and tell him she has returned and that he can come home this weekend to see her. Finally,

I lie down, and the white light of the moon streams onto the bed. I look at the moon and cry — out of gratitude, relief, and fear. This night I offer prayers for the small things that make a family, I offer prayers for the pain a family endures, I offer prayers for the strength that springs from unknown places, and finally, I pray for the future that, at this moment, in the pure glow of the moon, shines on all of us like nothing I've ever seen.

Skradena and the Candles

In memory of Mamie and Joe L. Ortiz, Misty and Lori's grandparents

The most popular version of the story about how luminarias originated is *The Farolitos of Christmas,* by renowned writer Rudolfo Anaya. Most communities have their own version of the popular Christmas story, and the following is an Acoma version.[5]

Not so long ago, they said, there was a little girl, Skradena—which means Corn Pollen—who lived in the Acoma village of McCartys. Skradena was five years old and lived with her grandparents.

Each year before Christmas, Skradena and her grandpa went south to the mesa of Tah gah yah, Black Mesa, to gather wood for the luminarias. They left early each afternoon, when it was the warmest, and returned two or three hours later, the wagon loaded with wood. Before supper, they unloaded the wood, and Grandpa chopped it into two-foot lengths. Skradena stacked the wood into small circles beginning at the dirt road leading to their house. Each day they added eight to ten piles. By Christmas Eve, the small wood piles lined both sides of the road up to the front porch of the house.

Skradena looked forward to this each year because as she and Grandpa went out each afternoon, he would tell her about the birth of Jesus. "Ba-ba, Grandpa," she would say, as soon as they climbed into the wagon, "tell me about Baby Jesus. Tell me, my Ba-ba." He would smile and begin talking in a low, quiet voice. Soon his talking and the rhythm of the horses' hooves filled the bright winter afternoon.

"Ba-ba," he would start, "long ago on the other side of the world, far away, people were very unhappy. It seemed that everyone argued with one another, and sometimes people would speak badly of others for no reason. People watched each other with contempt and grew jealous over possessions. The adults planned and plotted to hurt others they thought had caused their misfortune. Some parents did not care for their children, so young boys and girls roamed, stealing food, clothes, and other things to survive. Their behavior was frightening. Their parents attended to their own desires and needs, not knowing or caring where the children went. Nevertheless, some families did not succumb to these changes, and they stayed together and prayed as all people once had been taught. It seemed that a huge unhappiness had descended upon everyone and everything. Yet these people knew deep within their hearts that they were meant to live happily, that their lives should be filled with love, joy, and the strength that faith brings. Once, long ago, they had lived in that way. They felt so empty inside. So although the sun shone and plants grew, these natural gifts did not bring happiness and gratitude as before.

"Ba-ba, my grandchild," he continued, "word soon spread that a baby would be born who would bring joy and restore peace to the people. Although they were sad and unhappy, faces brightened at the thought of being lifted out of their misery. Some prayed together in groups, and others prayed alone in silence. Still others jeered and teased those who believed that a baby could save the world. The families who had always faithfully believed prayed fervently that the miracle would occur.

"One cold winter night, it happened. Three men who were herding sheep followed a brilliant, extraordinary star, and their sheep trailed after them in the bright desert light. As you know, Ba-ba, they were led to the corral where Baby Jesus lay. He was born there because his mother and father had no other place to stay. It was a cold night, and yet there he was—a little, chubby baby who taught all of us how to love one another and to care for each other. My little Ba-ba, Baby Jesus taught all people to treat each other with kindness, to share what we have, and to be good to our parents. All of the people learned again to appreciate others, even those they didn't agree with, and to realize that animals, the land, and all living things are important. Remember, Ba-ba, that some animals were in the stable when Baby Jesus was born. Maybe in their own language, they tell the story on Christmas Eve, too."

"That night, Ba-ba, my grandpa, the stars looked like fires, no? They were bright and sparkling."

"That's why we light luminarias, Ba-ba. We light the path up to our front door for the Christ Child. We will never turn him away from our home. This is how we say welcome to our home, Jesus, and bless us."

Skradena's grandpa told this story every year and on Christmas Eve, the dirt road leading to their home sparkled with little bonfires. Above, in the night sky, millions of stars glistened far away in the clear darkness. All families in the village believed as Skradena's family did, and so the whole village was aglow on Christmas Eve. After midnight mass, people visited one another, bringing baskets of fruit, nuts, and candy. The scents of chile stew, baked bread, coffee, and pies filled the warm houses. Christmas trees sparkled in the living rooms. They sang carols and told stories, then returned to their homes happy and tired. By sunrise, the fires burned to the ground, leaving black circles evenly spaced from the road to the front doors.

Then one winter Grandpa fell ill, and as Christmas approached, Skradena worried and prayed. She felt bad for Grandma, who so enjoyed the luminarias. Sometimes her eyes filled with tears as they stood on the front porch admiring the luminarias. But now Grandpa was too sick to go and get wood, and Skradena was too little to go out alone. Skradena worried about Grandpa, the luminarias, and most of all, about Grandma not seeing them on Christmas Eve. Grandpa had already talked with her and explained that the next year they would prepare the luminarias as usual.

That day she could think of nothing else. She thought there might be extra wood. But the wood already cut was needed for cooking and heating. Besides, she was not allowed to use an axe. She sat in the kitchen trying to figure what to do when she saw a box of candles beside the sewing machine—the votive candles Grandma used at church. She took one outside and lit it, but the cold wind quickly blew it out. But when she cupped her hands around it, it stayed lit. Then she realized her lunch bags were perfect. So she put some sand in the sacks and lined the road, placing the small brown sacks every three steps. This took most of the afternoon, and she would tell Grandma only that she was working on a surprise. Grandma saw her squatting beside the road, intensely busy with paper sacks. She smiled and told Grandpa, "Our little Corn Pollen is up to something and she won't tell me what."

That evening after supper, Skradena ran out, bundled in her jacket, and with her Uncle Gilly's help, they lit the little candles. When they came home, the sun had gone down. Grandma met them at the door and hugged Skradena and Gilly. "Thank you so much, Da uh, my sweet granddaughter. Thank you," she said, tears in her eyes. They helped Grandpa to the front door so that he could see the luminarias. He laughed with happiness. He held Skradena for a long time and thanked her and Gilly for making it possible for the Christ Child to come to their home.

It is said that this is how modern luminarias, using paper sacks and candles, began. Each Christmas Eve, luminarias line the highway to old Acoma. Brightly lit, evenly spaced lights begin at the top of the mesa and dip into the valley, then wind up the narrow road to the church at the top.

The church itself is outlined in luminarias. The distance from the mesa to Sky City is about five miles, and it is a breathtaking sight. The nights are clear and cold, and there are no electric lights, so the luminarias are glimmering fires, lighting the way once again for the Christ Child's visit. They light the path again in the same way that little Corn Pollen created.

A Birthday Poem

This morning, the sunrise is a brilliant song
cradling tiny birds and brittle leaves. The world
responds, stretching, humming. The sunlight is Diyin,
sacred beams as the Holy Ones arrive with prayers.
They bring gifts in the cold dawn. Again, as a Diné
woman, I face east on the porch and pray for Hózhó

one more time. For today, allow me to share Hózhó,
the beauty of all things being right and proper as in songs
the Holy Ones gave us. They created the world,
instilling stories and lessons so we would know Diyin
surrounds us. Our lives were set by precise prayers
and stories to ensure balance. Grant me the humor Diné

elders relish so. No matter what, let the Diné
love of jokes, stories, and laughter create some Hózhó.
Some days, even after great coffee, I need to hear a song
to reassure me that the distance from Dinétah is not a world
away. I know the soft hills, plains, and wind are Diyin
also. Yet I plan the next trip when we will say prayers

in the dim driveway. As we drive, Kansas darkens. Prayers
and memories protect us. In the tradition of Diné
travel, we eat, laugh, refuel, sing. Twice in Texas, Hózhó
arose in clear air above the flatness. The full moon was a song

we watched all night. We marveled at how quietly the world
is blessed. After midnight, Lori asks about the Diyin

Diné'é who dance in the Night Way ceremony. The sacred Diyin
Diné'é come after the first frost glistens. Their prayers
and long rhythmic songs help us live. This is a Diné
way of communion and cleansing. At the Night Way, Hózhó
awaits as we come to listen and absorb the songs
until they live within. It is true that the world

is restored by the Holy Ones who return to the Fourth World
to take part in the Night Way. They want to know that Diyin
still exists amongst their children. Their stories and prayers
guide us now. At times, the Holy Ones feared the Diné
would succumb to foreign ways. For them, it is truly Hózhó
to see us at the Night Way gathered in the smoky cold. Songs

rise with fire smoke. I tell Lori we Diné are made of prayers.
At times, the world may overwhelm us, yet because of the Diyin,
each morning we pray to restore Hózhó, Hózhó, Hózhó, Hózhó.

All the Colors of Sunset

Even after all this time, when I look back at all that happened, I don't know if I would do anything differently. That summer morning seemed like any other. The sun came up over the mountain around seven or so, and when I went to throw the coffee grounds out, I put the pouch of corn pollen in my apron pocket so that I could pray before I came inside.

During the summers, we sleep most nights in the chaha'oh, the shade-house, unless it rains. I remembered early that morning I had heard loud voices yelling and they seemed to come from the north. Whoever it was quieted quickly, and I fell back asleep. Right outside the chaha'oh, I knew the dogs were alert—their ears erect and eyes glistening. Out here near Rockpoint, where we live, it's so quiet and isolated that we can hear things from a far distance. It's mostly desert, and the huge rocks nearby—tséni-tsaadeez'áhí and the other rocks—seem to bounce noises into the valley. People live far apart and there are no streetlights nearby. The nights are quiet, except for animal and bird noises, and the sky is always very black. In the Navajo way, they say the night sky is made of black jet and that the folding darkness comes from the north. Sometimes in the evenings, I think of this when the sun is setting, and all the bright colors fall some-where into the west. Then I let the beauty of the sunset go, and my sadness along with it.

That morning I fixed a second pot of coffee and peeled potatoes to fry. Just as I finished slicing the potatoes, I thought I heard my grandbaby cry. I went out and looked out toward my daughter's home. She lives across the arroyo a little over a mile away. I shaded my eyes and squinted—the sun was already so bright. I didn't see anyone. I stood there awhile listening and looking in her direction. Finally, I went inside and finished fixing breakfast. We were going to go into Chinle that afternoon, so I didn't go over to their house.

Later that morning, I was polishing some pieces of jewelry when I heard my daughter crying outside. My heart quickened. I rushed to the door, and she practically fell inside the house. She was carrying the baby in her cradleboard and could hardly talk—she was sobbing and screaming so. I grabbed the baby, knowing she was hurt. When I looked at my granddaughter, I knew the terrible thing that had happened. Her little face was so pale and wet from crying. I could not think or speak. Somehow I found my way to the south wall of the hooghan and sat down, still holding my sweet baby. My first and only grandchild was gone.

I held her close and nuzzled her soft neck, I sang over and over the little songs that I always sang to her, and I unwrapped her and touched slowly, slowly every part of her little smooth body. I wanted to remember every sweet detail and said aloud each name like I had always done. "Díí nijáád wolyé, shi awéé'. This is called your leg, my baby." I asked her, "Nitsiiyah shą'?" and nuzzled the back of her neck like before. "Jó kwe'é." This time she did not giggle and laugh. I held her and rocked and sang and talked to her.

The pollen pouch was still in my pocket, and I put a bit into her mouth as I would have done when her first tooth came in. I put a pinch of pollen on her head as I would have done when she first left for kindergarten. I put a pinch of pollen in her little hands as I would have done when she was given her first lamb, as I would have done when she was given her own colt. This way she would have been gentle and firm with her pets. I brushed her with an eagle feather as I would have done when she graduated from junior high. All this, and so much more that could have been, swept over me as I sat there leaning over my little grandbaby.

She was almost five months old and had just started to recognize me. She cried for me to hold her, and I tried to keep her with me as much as I could. Sometimes I took her for long walks and showed her everything and told her little stories about the birds and animals we saw. She would fall asleep on our way home, and still I hummed and sang softly. I couldn't stop singing. For some reason, when she was born, I was given so much time for her. I guess that's how it is with grandparents. I wasn't ever too busy to care for her. When my daughter took her home, my house seemed so empty and quiet.

They said that I kept the baby for four hours that morning. My daughter left and then returned with her husband. They were afraid to bother me in my grief. I don't remember much of it. I didn't know how I acted, or maybe that was the least of what I was conscious of. My daughter said later that I didn't say one word to her. I don't remember.

Finally, I got up and gave the baby to them so they could go to the hospital at Chinle. I followed in my own truck, and when we got there the doctor confirmed her death. We began talking about what we had to do next. Word spread quickly. When I went to buy some food at Bashas', several people comforted me and helped me with the shopping. My sisters and two aunts were at my home when I returned. They had straightened up the house and were cooking already. Some of my daughter's in-laws were cooking and getting things ready in the chaha'oh outside. By that evening, the house and the chaha'oh were filled with people—our own relatives, clan relatives, friends from school and church, and the baby's father's kin. People came and held me, comforting me and murmuring their sympathies. They cried with me and brought me plates of food. I felt like I was in a daze. I hardly spoke. I tried to help cook and serve but was gently guided back to the armchair that had somehow become "my chair" since that morning.

There were meetings each day, and various people stood up to counsel and advise everyone who was there, including my daughter and her husband. When everything was done, and we had washed our faces and started over again, I couldn't seem to focus on things. Before all this had happened, I was very busy each day—cooking, sewing, taking out the horses sometimes, feeding the animals, and often just visiting with people. One of my children or my sisters always came by, and we would talk and laugh while I continued my tasks. Last winter was a good year for piñons, so I was still cleaning and roasting the many flour sackfuls we had picked. At Manyfarms junction, some people from Shiprock had a truckload of the sweetest corn I had ever tasted, so I bought plenty and planned to make nitsidigo'í and other kinds of cornbread. We would have these tasty delicacies to eat in the winter. We liked to remember summer by the food we had stored and preserved.

When we were little, my mother taught all of us girls to weave, but I hadn't touched a loom in years. When I became a grandmother, I began to think of teaching some of the old things to my baby. Maybe it was my age, but I remembered a lot of the things we were told. Maybe it was that I was alone more than I had ever been—my children were grown and my husband had passed on five years before—and since I was by myself and I had enough to live on, I stopped working at a paying job.

After all this happened, I resumed my usual tasks and tried to stay busy so that my grandbaby's death wouldn't overwhelm me. I didn't cry or grieve out loud because they say that one can call the dead back by doing that. Yet so much had changed, and it was as if I was far away from everything. Some days I fixed a lunch and took the sheep out for the day and returned as the sun was going down. And when I came back inside, I realized that I hadn't spoken to the animals all day. It seemed strange, and yet I just didn't feel like talking. The dogs would follow me around, wanting attention—for me to throw a stick for them or talk to them; then after a while they would just lie down and watch me. Once I cleaned and roasted a pan of piñons perfectly without thinking about it. It's a wonder that I didn't burn myself. A few weeks later, we had to brand some colts and give the horses shots, so everyone got together and we spent the day at the corral in the dust and heat. Usually, it was a happy and noisy time, but that day was quieter than usual. At least we had taken care of everything.

Sometimes I dreamt of my grandbaby, and it was as if nothing had happened. In my dreams, I carried her around, singing and talking to her. She smiled and giggled at me. When I awoke, it was as if she had been lying beside me, kicking and reaching around. A small space beside me would be warm, and her scent faint. These dreams seemed so real. I looked forward to sleeping because maybe in sleeping I might see her. On the days following such a dream, I would replay it over and over in my mind, still smiling and humming to her the next morning. By afternoon, the activity and noise had usually worn the dream off.

I heard after the funeral that people were whispering and asking questions about what had happened. It didn't bother me. Nothing anyone said or did would bring my sweet baby back—that was clear. I never asked my daughter how it happened. After the baby's death, she and her husband became very quiet, and they were together so much that they seemed like shadows of each other. Her husband worked at different jobs, and she just went with him and waited in the pickup until he was through. He worked with horses, helped build hooghans and corrals, and did other construction work. When she came over and spent the afternoon with me, we hardly talked. We both knew we were more comfortable that way. As usual, she hugged me each time before she left. I knew she was in great pain.

Once, when I was at Bashas' shopping for groceries, a woman I didn't know said to me, "You have a pretty grandbaby." I smiled and didn't reply. I noticed that she didn't say "yę́ę" at the end of "nisóí," which means "the grandbaby who is no longer alive." That happened at other places, and I didn't respond, except to smile. I thought it was good that people remembered her.

About four months after her death, we were eating at my house when my sisters gathered around me and told me that they were very worried about me. They thought I was still too grief-stricken over the baby and that it was not healthy. "You have to let her go," they said. They said they wanted the "old me" back, so I agreed to go for help.

We went to a medicine woman near Ganado, and she asked me if I could see the baby sometimes. No, I said, except in dreams.

"Has anyone said they've seen her?" she asked. I said that I didn't think so. Then she said, "Right now, I see the baby beside you." I was so startled that I began looking around for her.

"The baby hasn't left," she said. "She wants to stay with you." I couldn't see my grandbaby. Then I realized that other people could see what the medicine woman had just seen. No wonder, I thought, that sometimes when I awoke, I could feel her little warm body beside me. She said the baby was wrapped in white.

She couldn't help me herself, but she told me to see another medicine person near Lukachukai. She said that the ceremony I needed was very old and that she didn't know it herself. The man she recommended was elderly and very knowledgeable, and so it was likely that he would know the ceremony, or would at least know of someone who did.

Early in the morning, we went to his house west of Many Farms. Word had already been sent that we were coming. The ceremony lasted for four days and three nights, and parts of songs and prayers had such ancient sacred words I wasn't sure if I understood them. When the old man prayed and sang, sometimes tears streamed down my face as I repeated everything after him, word for word, line for line, late into the night. We began again at daybreak. I was exhausted and so relieved. I finally realized what my grief had done. I could finally let my grandbaby go.

We were lucky that we found this old man, because the ceremony had not been done in almost eighty years. He had seen it as a little boy and had memorized all the parts of it—the songs, the advice, the prayers, and the literal letting go of the dead spirit. Over time, it had become a rare ceremony, because what I had done in holding and keeping the baby for those hours was not in keeping with the Diné way. I understood that doing so had upset the balance of life and death. When we left, we were all crying. I thanked the old man for his memory, his life, and his ability to help us when no one could. I understand now that all of life has ceremonies connected with it, and for us, without our memory, our old people, and our children, we would be like lost people in this world we live in, as well as in the other worlds in which our loved ones are waiting.

She Was Singing in the Early Morning

I was in Shiprock recently, and one evening my family and extended family orchestrated a big dinner for me. The evening was noisy and filled with laughter. They gave this dinner because I was home from Kansas and obviously deprived of many things, mainly food, that are necessary for a normal Navajo lifestyle. As we ate, everyone took turns telling about what had happened to them or about news they had heard since my last visit.

The next day, Gloria, a first cousin (therefore my sister) and I gathered up a couple of the kids to go with us to Durango where I was to read at Fort Lewis College. Luckily, the children were on spring break. At Shiprock, it feels lonely to go anywhere without one or two little ones in the back seat or squirming around in the pickup. We talked and laughed all the way, hardly listening to the radio. My sister drove while I finished putting on my makeup. Another sister's boys, our sons, watched intently from the back seat and asked me questions like "What's that?" or "What does that do?" and "What would happen if you didn't wear makeup?" Sometimes I answered their questions. Once or twice I simply turned around and looked at them. "Oops," they'd say under their breaths, smiling.

At Fort Lewis, I read a poem that included a Navajo song, along with other poems and stories. Afterwards, Gloria said, "You can really sing, Nízhóní ya." Then she said, "I hardly sing anymore." "What do you mean?" I asked. It is hard to imagine her or any of my sisters not singing.

My image of all my sisters intertwines with music and singing. In high school, we liked to sing out loud with the radio. Sometimes when we were riding with my brothers or out on a double date, one of our favorite songs would come on the car radio. We insisted that the driver pull off the road, while we jumped out and danced alongside the road until the song was over. My brothers would not dance; instead, they stood there disgusted until we got back into the truck. Our dates usually cooperated out of shock. When Gloria went to boarding school, she and other Navajo girls sang traditional songs late at night after the lights were turned out. She would lie on the top bunk staring at the huge silver water tank outside and imagine the long summer nights when such songs are sung until early morning. She remembered the times she and her friends darted between the cars, parked in a huge circle, trying to track down a handsome guy, or the times she heard the songs when she was helping out in the chaha'oh where they cooked and fed people all night. She learned a lot of songs that year. "We were lonely, I guess," she said.

Recently, while driving on the turnpike to Topeka, I was singing with the radio and my daughter said, "You sound like my other mom," meaning Gloria. I smiled. I felt happy when she said that.

Now as we rounded a steep mountain curve in Colorado, I asked her, "How come you stopped singing?"

She said, "Remember what Thomas did to me when I ended up in the hospital? He tried to choke me, and it did something to my voice box. Since that happened, I sound awful when I sing." We all fell silent. Outside the moving car, tall pine trees stood still, glistening as the sunlight sparkled through the thick wet branches. It had rained lightly that afternoon.

"It's a good thing you left him," I said.

Early the next morning at Gloria's house, I heard her preparing breakfast in the kitchen. I slept in the room of her daughter who is attending college in Colorado. I could hear her pouring water for coffee, followed by the rhythmic peeling of potatoes. The house was quiet, and the sun rose brightly above Dziłná'oodiłii, a few miles to the east. I heard her humming softly. A few minutes later, I heard her singing. Her lilting voice drifted into the room where I lay. She was singing in the quiet, sunlit kitchen. She was singing as she mixed dough. She was singing because she thought no one could hear her.

Later, we ate a hot breakfast of eggs, potatoes, bacon, and náneeskaadí—hot tortillas. "This is so good," I said. Then her husband, Raymond, said, "She cooks like this every morning. It's really good to start every day like this. Out here on the rez, there's nothing to rush around for. Probably somewhere else, people rush out of their houses every morning without eating. We always see white people doing that on TV. Even though we don't have a lot out here, nihighan biih hóhzó—our home is full of happiness." Then he touched my sister's shoulder as he passed behind her chair.

That Guy

They said that there was a guy who went to Gallup for a late afternoon meeting, and afterwards he went with some colleagues to eat dinner before returning home to Window Rock. His buddies decided to hit a few bars first, and so he agreed to go along since he had ridden in with them. But the whole thing wasn't his idea. Anyway, the evening flew by, and they all had a good time going from place to place, dancing, and just talking to people. They were at the edge of town when the bars closed, and suddenly he couldn't find anyone he had come with.

He had no choice but to begin walking north toward Window Rock. In the cool early morning air, he became filled with remorse, for he knew everyat home would be mad at him. He could already hear his mother's scolding voice and feel the awful silent treatment, a behavior at which his wife excelled. Nevertheless, he trudged homeward looking tired and disheveled.

Much later, as he approached J.B. Tanner Trading Co., he remembered that the trader butchered sheep in the morning and that anyone who helped would be paid with fresh mutton. Like all good Diné men, he was an expert at butchering. In fact, he often bragged that he could butcher a sheep alone in thirty minutes. He decided to help out and that way, he surmised, his family wouldn't be so angry for his transgression. How could they stay mad if he walked in with a bag of fresh mutton?

He and a few others helped for an hour or so; then he set out again for Window Rock with two paper sacks of mutton tucked inside his jacket. He walked along a worn dirt trail at the bottom of the sloping side of the busy highway. To the west were small hills and valleys covered with large shrubs and piñon trees.

All of a sudden, on the highway above, a car broadsided a pickup, and both vehicles lost control. There was a lot of noise and activity, and since he couldn't see the highway from beneath, he wasn't aware of what happened. In the same instant, a hubcap from a car flew off and hurled downward, spinning as it struck him in the forehead. They said he was knocked unconscious immediately. He had no idea what happened. Soon there were a number of ambulances and police on the scene attending to the victims. No one knew he was lying down on the path. When he came to, he heard the sirens and loud voices, and he climbed a small hill and saw the flashing lights. "They found out!" he thought in his disoriented state. "My family told them I stayed out all night! Dooládó' doodada!" he cursed. He panicked and took off running into the hills away from the highway. He was sure they were after him.

Meanwhile, a policeman investigating the accident was walking around and picking up vehicle fragments. One of the sheriff's deputies saw the hubcap at the bottom of the slope and went down to retrieve it. Then he noticed a lot of blood around it and a bloody trail away from the scene. He was mystified because there were also some internal organs and bits of flesh and bone in the dirt. He followed the trail a ways, then noticed a man running faraway into the hills. The man was covered with blood, yet he was moving pretty quickly. The deputy was amazed that one so obviously injured would have the strength to walk, much less run.

Another policeman came down and said, "Was someone thrown out and landed down here?" "Yeah," the deputy said. "He took off running, too." The policemen watched the small figure moving quickly among the trees. "Boy, those Navajos sure are tough," the deputy said. "Yeah, they're something else," the other agreed as they surveyed the remains of that guy's mutton peace offering.

Sometimes on Summer Evenings

Nihidá'í, one of our mother's brothers, lived west of our home, and he
walked everywhere. He never owned a car. We often saw him approaching
at a distance. Sometimes he would cut across the field instead of taking the
bottom road alongside the fields. When we saw him, we called out, "'Aadi
nihidá'í yaash yigaał! Our mother's brother is coming!" We stopped every-
thing, and some children ran inside the house or the chaha'oh, the brush
shadehouse during the summer, and began putting coffee cups, bread,
and other food on the table. Others ran to meet him and walk back with
him, holding his hands, or hanging onto his back belt loop. Still others
darted frantically around the house looking in drawers and shelves, call-
ing out, "Tł'óółts'ósí ła, shimá! My mother, I need some string now!" All
the while, we called out over and over, "'Aadi nihidá'í yaash! Here comes
our mother's brother!" Our mother, or another adult, heated coffee and
prepared to feed him. When he arrived at the house, we children would
become very shy, but we stayed near him, fighting silently to sit on his
lap, some of us already seated and pressed against him. Still, we were too
bashful to speak. He would murmur to each of us, "My daughter, you've
grown. Do you help your mother, my baby? Sit here, my little one." We
would smile while looking at the ground. Nihidá'í did not speak English,
and he always seemed old because of his wise and gentle manner. While
he drank coffee and talked with the adults, we stayed nearby, sometimes
sitting at his feet. After it was clear the "serious" conversation was over,
one of us would hand two or three loops of cotton twine to nihidá'í.

   Nihidá'í was a master at telling and performing stories with string. As
he talked, little characters or land formations appeared and moved flaw-

lessly between his fingers as the story progressed. We were enthralled each time. We were invariably consistent in this request, even in the summertime, though we knew clearly that string stories should not be told in the summer. He would say, "Shúúh sha' áłchíní, shįįgo 'éi haní' doobaayajiłti'da. Listen, my children, these stories cannot be told in the summer. Remember that, my little ones." So he sang to us, bouncing us one at a time on his knee. He sang humorous songs about goats, donkeys, lambs, and other animals. In many of the songs, animal sounds were imitated, and we all made the noises together and laughed until our stomachs ached. When he left, the whole greeting process was repeated in saying farewell—the sudden shyness and quietness, the clinging and possessiveness, and the insistence on accompanying him, this time until he told us to return home. Inevitably, one or two kids had fallen asleep during the stories, so there were fewer kids to see him off but the same number of puppies and dogs.

It was clear nihidá'í loved us very much, though he never told us so. It was in his voice, his joy in seeing us, the way he endured our clinging hands, his pride in our presence. As we grew older, we often marveled at nihidá'í's patience during his visits. As our mother's brother, he was the quintessential "'adá'í" because he was responsible for our upbringing as much as our father was. In the Diné matrilineal culture, his role was to teach, guide, and discipline us. Thus we were careful not to do things that might be "reported" to nihidá'í; we couldn't bear to disappoint him or make him sad. Sometimes when we were unruly, my mother would say, "I hope that I won't have to tell my brother about any of you." She'd say this quietly, almost under her breath, and we became frightened. Sometimes our uncle watched us when my parents went on a trip, and we had such fun. He played with us, let us mess up the house, and essentially gave us all his attention. Much later, I learned that he was giving us "quality time." He had a family and children of his own, but when we were with him, we were "number one" to him. The same was true of our father's relationship with his nieces and nephews. Likewise, my mother had a number of relatives, and maybe friends, with whom she had close relationships. When she spoke of them, she often referred to them as her "sister" or "younger brother," as if they were her biological siblings. We knew who her "real" brothers and sisters were, but to consider people in these terms was to show love and respect for them. Therefore, we did not use English terms such as "cousin" or "uncle" for anyone. Such titles seemed to connote a distance that didn't exist. We understood kinship roles such as this very early, and it was hard to imagine being outside the security of such relationships.

Many years later, I wrote the following poem in tribute to nihidá'í yaash, who passed on in early 1985

HILLS BROTHERS COFFEE

My uncle is a small man.
In Navajo, we call him "shidá'í,"
        my mother's brother.

He doesn't know English,
        but his name in the white way is Tom Jim.
        He lives about a mile or so
        down the road from our house.

One morning he sat in the kitchen,
drinking coffee.

I just came over, he said.
The store is where I'm going to.

He tells me about how my mother seems to be gone
every time he comes over.
      Maybe she sees me coming
      then runs and jumps in her car
      and speeds away!
      he says smiling.

We both laugh—just to think of my mother
jumping in her car and speeding.

I pour him more coffee
and he spoons in sugar and cream
until it looks almost like a chocolate shake.
Then he sees the coffee can.
      Oh, that's that coffee with the man in a dress
      like a church man.
      Ah-h, that's the one that does it for me.
      Very good coffee.

I sit down again and he tells me,
      Some coffee has no kick.
      But this one is the one.
      It does it good for me.

I pour us both a cup
and while we wait for my mother,

his eyes crinkle with the smile and he says,
>   Yes, ah yes. This is the very one
>   (putting in more sugar and cream).

So I usually buy Hills Brothers Coffee.
Once or sometimes twice a day,
I drink a hot coffee and

>   it sure does it for me.[6]

Sometimes on summer evenings, we cooked outside over an open fire and then ate sitting around the fire or at a picnic table. As we ate, my father or another adult would begin "talking." This type of talking was different in tone and subject from ordinary conversation. We learned to remain quiet and still when they said "Nihizhé'é yáłti'—Your father is talking," or "Hazhó' ógoo sínídá háiida yádaałti'go—Sit quietly when someone is talking." They told stories about various ancestors or faraway relatives (whom we didn't see often), or they told about the stars and various astronomical bodies, or maybe they shared concerns or made plans. During these times, blankets were brought out for the little ones, and we sat wrapped up, or leaned against the nearest adult while the youngest ones eventually fell asleep on someone's lap and were carried to bed. Such summer evenings were filled with quiet voices, dogs barking far away, the fire crackling, and often we could hear the faint drums and songs of a ceremony somewhere in the distance. There were no electric lights, and the night sky was so very dark and black. While the adults talked, we lay wrapped in blankets and the stars seemed within reach. We could hear the horses snorting in nearby fields, frogs croaking, the tinkling of sheep bells, and the motor of an occasional passing car in the distance.

My childhood is intertwined with memories of various relatives "talking" to me and sharing by implication the value of silence, listening, and observation.[7]

They Moved over the Mountain

My mother was born at Rockpoint on the Arizona side of Beautiful Mountain in the Carriso Mountain range. While very young, she and her family—her mother, sister, two brothers, and stepfather—moved across the mountain to Niist'áá, herding the sheep and horses ahead of them.

Tsinaabąąs naaki bił jin naajin—They had two horse-drawn wagons that they used in the move. When they left, some relatives asked them to leave one of the wagons, for they were highly prized and hard to come by. After much discussion, my mother's family left with both wagons. Tsinaabąąs 'éí t'áá 'íighiís shimásanibí 'ídna, 'áko bídeezhí ła'shídó' nigoo ákóhóót'iid. The wagons belonged to my grandmother whose husband had bought them from a white man years before. But my grandmother's younger sister wanted one for herself and for the use of the other relatives who would remain at Rockpoint. Since they were sisters, she could make this claim.

My grandmother thought ahead to the futures of her teenage sons and eleven-year-old daughter, and she refused her sister's request. Besides, they would also need the wagons to haul logs and water when they built their hooghan and corrals at the new place. My own mother was still very small—maybe three years old.

So their departure was subdued and tinged with more sadness than usual because of this incident. Later on, her sister and others came to see them at Niist'áá, and the sisters cried when they saw each other. They were happy to be together again.

"T'ah ndi áníts'íísíigo ákodhodzaa, ákoh ayóó bénáshniih. Even though I was very little, I still remember this clearly," my mother said. "On the way over the mountain, the weeds and plants were very high. I could barely see because the weeds had grown higher than me in some places. I cried to walk, and they let me, but they had to keep an eye on me because I could easily get lost. I walked, separating a path ahead of me with my arms. I remember that I was very little and thought it was really something to walk alone in the tall plants."

This is a part of where my writing begins—one of my mother's earliest memories, a window into my past almost eight decades ago. These old stories allow me to imagine shimásání, my maternal grandmother, and shicheii, my maternal grandfather, both of whom died several decades before I was born. This is, for me, a "way of looking," both at the present and at what is yet to come.

Blue Horses Rush In

For Chamisa Bah Edmo, Shisóí 'aláąjį' naaghígíí

Before the birth, she moved and pushed inside her mother.
Her heart pounded quickly and we recognized
the sound of horses running:
> the thundering of hooves on the desert floor.

Her mother clenches her fists and gasps.
She moans ageless pain and pushes: This is it!

Chamisa slips out, glistening wet, and takes her first breath.
> The wind outside swirls small leaves
> and branches in the dark.
Her father's eyes are wet with gratitude.
He prays and watches both mother and baby—stunned.

This baby arrived amid a herd of horses,
> horses of different colors.

White horses ride in on the breath of the wind.
White horses from the east
where plants of golden chamisa shimmer in the moonlight.

She arrived amid a herd of horses.

Blue horses enter from the south
bringing the scent of prairie grasses
from the small hills outside.

She arrived amid a herd of horses.

Yellow horses rush in, snorting from the desert in the west.
It is possible to see across the entire valley to Niist'áá from Tó.
Bah, from here your grandmothers went to war long ago.

She arrived amid a herd of horses.

Black horses came from the north.
They are the lush summers of Montana and still white winters of Idaho.

Chamisa, Chamisa Bah. It is all this that you are.
You will grow: laughing, crying,
and we will celebrate each change you live.

You will grow strong like the horses of your past.
You will grow strong like the horses of your birth.

Notes

1. "Hohokamki" is the Tohono O'odham name of the people now commonly called "Hohokam."

2. Commissioned by the Phoenix Arts Commission, the City of Phoenix, Arizona, 1990.

3. This piece was originally published by Helicon Nine. Feuillet. Kansas City, Missouri, 1994, 4 pages. Original copyright is retained by author.

4. Li-Young Lee, "Furious Versions" appeared in *The City in Which I Love You,* published by BOA Editions, Brockport, Massachusetts, 1990, page 26.

5. An altered version of this story appeared in the *Lawrence Journal World,* 24 December 1995, page 3D.

6. This poem originally appeared in *Sáanii Dahataal: The Women Are Singing,* published by The University of Arizona Press, Tucson, 1993, pages 27–28.

7. This piece is an excerpt from a longer essay to be published in *Everything Matters,* edited by Brian Swann and Arnold Krupat for Random House, New York, to be published in 1997.

About the Author

Luci Tapahonso is originally from Shiprock, New Mexico, and now teaches at the University of Kansas in Lawrence. She is the author of four other books of poetry, the most recent of which is *Sáanii Dahataał / The Women Are Singing: Poems and Stories,* also part of the Sun Tracks series in American Indian literature and published by the University of Arizona Press.